"You must come back to Barazbin. I am the sole heir." He resisted the urge to tell her that their marriage must provide heirs for the country. That was a given fact.

She shook her head. "No, Kazim, that's never going to happen."

He sighed impatiently. "I am concerned for our people. Your absence has brought my ability to rule into doubt. You *will* come back with me. Do you understand?"

Irritation surged through Amber, instantly replacing the softer emotion she'd felt for Kazim as he'd told her about his father. "Oh, I understand, Kazim. You think you can send me away and order me back at your whim. I don't feel like your wife, Kazim. It has been ten months since we married and this is the first time I have seen you."

All the hurt and anger she'd kept inside her since that night bubbled up, giving her the confidence to face the man who had broken her heart and shattered her foolish dreams.

"We married out of duty, Amber—never forget that." His calm voice was full of authority, his expression harsh and forbidding. "And now my duty is to return to Barazbin—with you."

Rachael Thomas has always loved reading romance and is thrilled to now be a Harlequin Presents author. She lives and works on a farm in Wales, a far cry from the glamour of a Presents story, but that makes slipping into her characters' world all the more appealing. When she's not writing or working on the farm, she enjoys photography and visiting historic castles and grand houses. Visit her at rachaelthomas.co.uk.

Other titles by Rachael Thomas available in ebook:

A DEAL BEFORE THE ALTAR

Rachael Thomas

———

Claimed by the Sheikh

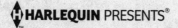

Recycling programs
for this product may
not exist in your area.

ISBN-13: 978-0-373-13795-4

Claimed by the Sheikh

First North American Publication 2015

Copyright © 2015 by Rachael Thomas

This is a work of fiction. Names, characters, places and incidents are
either the product of the author's imagination or are used fictitiously,
and any resemblance to actual persons, living or dead, business
establishments, events or locales is entirely coincidental.

This edition published by arrangement with Harlequin Books S.A.

For questions and comments about the quality of this book,
please contact us at CustomerService@Harlequin.com.

Printed in U.S.A.

Claimed by the Sheikh

For Kate Walker and Sharon Kendrick
whose inspiring and encouraging courses
have helped me enormously.

PROLOGUE

THIS WAS THE moment Amber had been looking forward to. Her wedding day. Her new husband, Prince Kazim Al Amed of Barazbin, was powerful and, despite her nerves, Amber wanted their first night together to be perfect. He might be the man her father had chosen for her to marry, but she'd given her heart to him the moment they'd first met. His reputation preceded him and she intended to hide her virginal innocence by playing the role of seductress to perfection.

As soon as they'd left the wedding feast things had changed, had gone wrong. His warm smile had disappeared and he stood in their suite, anger clouding his handsome face.

'I have no wish for this marriage.' He almost had to force the word 'marriage' out. 'There is no need to change your life.'

'Change my life?' How could he so calmly say that? Of course her life would change, but she held her chin high, kept her strength, not wanting to appear weak to a man so strong.

'Like you, I have married out of duty and respect for my family.' His eyes, as black as obsidian, fixed on hers and a sizzle of something indefinable raced down her spine. She clenched her fingers tightly beneath the silk of her *abaya*.

He picked up her hand; the warmth of his fingers around hers made her heart race and for a moment she saw confusion in his eyes.

'We have done our duty. Now you will return to your family.'

Kazim breathed a sigh of relief, thankful his bride was a level-headed woman not prone to hysteria. It must be the Western influence she'd had in her life. The same influence that had corrupted her. Rumours of her secret assignations with men in hotel rooms whilst at boarding school had only just reached his ears. She was not the innocent bride he had been expecting. He had done his duty, married the woman his father had selected. He would do no more.

'So what must I do?' She looked panicked for a moment and he wondered if his assumptions had been premature.

'Whatever it was you were doing before you arrived here. You will, of course, have my full financial support.' As far as he was concerned,

after what he'd just learnt he had every right to
send his new wife home and then one day call
into question her suitability.

'So I just go back to my life?'

'There is one problem.' He hesitated. 'It will
be expected for the marriage to be consummated.'

'That's easily sorted.' She jumped up impetu-
ously and tugged at her *abaya*, pulling the long
lengths of silk. 'We can make it look as if it has.'

Kazim couldn't believe what he was hearing
and seeing. As each piece of silk was removed
and tossed aside lust thudded through his veins.
This woman was his wife, an innocent virgin,
but she was performing some kind of striptease.
What had she learnt in England?

With each movement she became bolder,
seducing him with her curves, her sexy pout.
Anger mixed with disbelief was making a heady
cocktail. This woman was no innocent. But still
he watched as lust thundered in his blood.

The silk ripped as her movements became
faster and she gasped, her face full of genuine
shock. Then she smiled. The smile of a woman
who knew how to tease a man. 'That will make
it look all the more real.'

Then the last piece of silk slipped to the floor,
leaving her almost naked, and their eyes met.
She stood and looked at him, as if daring him

to resist her now. He was hardly able to, but taking her now was out of the question. His rage was so strong he knew what could happen and he couldn't risk that.

'Put some clothes on,' he growled, hardly able to contain the anger he felt. In just a few minutes she'd proved herself completely unsuitable as his bride.

A short while later she emerged from the bathroom, her lush body covered by the soft towelling robe. She sat on the bed, her rich coffee eyes meeting his in challenge. 'The bed will need to look as if we've slept together in it.'

'What?'

She calmly sat there, her breasts rising and falling with each breath, making it harder than ever to resist the call of his lust.

'The bed,' she said coldly. 'If you want this marriage to look as if it has been consummated, it needs to be a mess.'

Amber watched the man she'd married toss the sheets into disarray and self-preservation kicked in. She wasn't about to be sent home a disgraced bride, one who was still a virgin. It had to look as if the marriage had been consummated. She couldn't face her parents otherwise.

If her husband could be as cold and calculating about the marriage they'd entered into out of duty, then so could she. The deal struck by their fathers would be honoured, as long as it looked as if they'd spent the night in the same bed.

Just a few more hours and she could leave. Go as far away as she could. Maybe go places and do things her position as her father's only daughter and Princess of Quarazmir had never enabled her to do.

CHAPTER ONE

Ten months later

HE'D FOUND HER.

Prince Kazim Al Amed of Barazbin had found her.

Amber watched as he made his way across the Parisian club, striding between the tables, scanning the dancers. Even in the dim light she could see the contempt on his face and the seductive beat of the music hardly slowed his pace. If anything, it increased it.

Rooted to the spot, she couldn't move. She didn't want to watch him but couldn't stop herself. Every step he took radiated command, accentuating the raw masculine power that served only to highlight his untamed nature. His tanned complexion, glossy black hair and expensive suit made him stand out against the club's regular clientele, and she certainly wasn't the only person to have noticed him.

A tremor of nerves, mixing with the same attraction she'd felt when they'd first met, raced through her. She clutched the tray of glasses she'd been collecting even tighter, desperate to stop them clinking together. For almost a year she'd dreamt he'd seek her out and declare his love but, from the look on his face, she knew such hopes were futile.

He had never loved her and she dreaded his reason for being here. She wasn't sure she could take another brutal rejection from the man she'd loved once with such adoration. He had been her dream come true. The only man she had ever loved.

Thankful the sultry lighting in the club would enable her to slip away virtually unnoticed, she put down the tray and, without taking her eyes from his tall body, moved backwards into the shadows. The music thumped as wildly as her heart when she saw him pause, his brow furrowed into a suspicious frown as he stood rigid and tall. His eyes rested briefly on her and she couldn't help but hold his gaze.

Kazim took one step towards her and she thought the game was up. Then he looked around the club once more and relief washed over her. He hadn't recognised her. She should be glad, but a dart of pain stabbed at her.

Just when she thought she could breathe again, his gaze returned once more to her, this time with unnerving accuracy. He took another step towards her, oblivious to the customers and waitresses trying to pass him, his piercing gaze not leaving her face. Judging by the tight line of his lips and the firmness of his jaw, he knew it was her and wasn't pleased.

Amber's hands shot up to her hair, checking the blonde, pink-streaked wig she used at work was in place. Surely he hadn't recognised her like this—had he? But she wasn't about to take any chances. She wasn't ready to face him yet—not here, not like this. She needed time to compose herself, time to put aside all the dreams he'd shattered.

Kazim looked once more at the dancers then back at her. The distance between them suddenly closed, even though neither had moved, and she felt his suspicion and shock with every nerve in her body. She had to go. Right now.

Quickly, she moved between the customers, seeing only the door to the dressing rooms. The door to sanctuary and, hopefully, escape. She couldn't face him yet. She needed time to find her strength.

She pushed open the heavy door, rushing along the narrow corridor towards the dressing rooms, her eyes blinking against the bright lights. Her heart pounded; she couldn't believe he was here, not after his cruel words to her that one and only night they'd spent together.

'Amber.' His accented voice rang with command, leaving her in no doubt that he had recognised her.

She froze. Her name on his lips, so full of authority, she didn't dare move. She couldn't even turn around. Her heart galloped faster than a racehorse as she heard his footsteps behind her on the tiled floor, coming closer, until a shiver of something she refused to acknowledge ran down her spine. How could he still have that effect on her?

The door to the club closed, muffling the beat of the music, and all she could hear was the tap of expensive leather shoes on the tiled floor. Then silence. She knew he stood almost right behind her. She could feel him, her whole body aware of his, but still she couldn't turn.

Finally her feet were able to move and she hurried on towards the dressing rooms, not looking back. She didn't dare. One look at him would unleash all the memories of her spoiled dreams. Dreams he had crushed.

'You can run, Amber, but you can't hide.' The undercurrent of steel in his voice made her stop just as she reached the dressing room door. Slowly she turned, knowing the time had come, whether she liked it or not—this was the moment she'd dreaded for almost a year.

It was time to face her past.

'I'm not running.' The words rushed out boldly as she looked into his face. She surprised herself with the courage in them.

As Amber looked at Kazim she lifted her chin and pushed her shoulders back. He'd changed. He was still undeniably handsome, but different. She watched him take a few more paces towards her. The severe fluorescent light of the narrow corridor highlighted the angles of his face, the slant of his cheekbones and the firm set of his lips. She had to hold her ground now. She couldn't let him see how unnerved she was. 'Neither am I trying to hide, Kazim.'

'I don't think you can do much hiding in that ridiculous thing.' His black eyes blazed with fury as he looked at her wig.

She couldn't help herself and reached up again to touch it. 'Part of the job,' she said flippantly as he came to stand directly in front of her and way too close. His annoyance at the wig pleased her, fuelling much needed resistance to him.

His gaze snapped back to hers, his contempt washing over her, just as it had done when she'd last seen him. Images replayed frantically in her mind, as clear as if it had all happened last night instead of many months ago.

That night he'd rejected her, rebuffed her clumsy advances and scorned her love. He'd turned her away without a second thought of what it would mean to her, not caring how such a dismissal would affect her. Because of that, she was now a different woman to the one she had been that night. She had to be stronger. She *was* stronger. He wouldn't hurt her again.

'And this?' He reached out, his fingers plucking at the feathers which adorned the bottom of her corset-style outfit, bringing her sharply back to the present. She wanted to jump quickly away from the heat of his touch but refused to give into the urge. 'Is this part of the job too?'

'Yes,' she snapped, roughly brushing his hand away. She would never let him know how he'd hurt her, how he'd destroyed her life. 'What I do for a living is no longer any of your concern. You made sure of that.'

Indignation simmered inside her as she remembered how he'd sent her away, turned his back on her as if she could just return to her life and it would all be the same. In reality, it had changed beyond comprehension and he hadn't cared.

His posture stiffened, making him appear taller, dominating the small space. 'A living? You call this a living?' Dark eyes, glittering with barely concealed anger, pierced hers, as if trying to extract every secret from her soul.

'Don't worry.' She put her hands on her hips and glared at him, exasperated at his obvious scorn for her. 'Nobody knows who I really am.'

She didn't know who she was any more, managing to convince herself, as well as her flatmate, that she was just a regular girl trying to earn a living and get over a broken heart.

'That explains why you were so hard to find.' Irritation filled his voice, but it didn't matter; she knew what his presence at the club meant.

'It was never my intention to be found.' She glowered at him as anger pushed aside those futile flutters of hope. 'I have moved on.'

'To a dubious lifestyle like this?' The mockery in his voice was painfully clear, but she wouldn't let him crush her dreams, not a second time.

'I have plans, Kazim. I've signed up for an art course.' As soon as she said the words she wished she could snatch them back.

He took a deep breath, as if seeking patience. 'What of your duty?'

'Duty?' She almost spat the word at him. 'What was it you said on our wedding night? Oh, yes—*We have done our duty. Now you will return to your family.*'

She stood and looked at him, those words

echoing in her head. For a moment foolish hope soared in her heart, hope that he had realised he did love her, but quickly she quashed it, locking it away. He was not here because he loved her. Why was he here, when he'd made it blatantly obvious he wanted nothing to do with her? That it was a marriage to be endured and one she suspected he would like to extricate himself from.

The harsh expression on his face kept her silent. The same intensely black eyes she'd fallen so rapidly in love with now glittered with bitter gold sparks as he looked at her. 'I cannot believe you have hidden yourself away in Paris, especially not this part of the city.'

'So you'd rather I'd have broadcast to the world I was here, would you?' Defiant words hit their target and a sense of satisfaction filled her as she saw Kazim's jaw clench. She watched fury highlight the gold in his eyes. If he thought he could just waltz back into her life and make judgements on what she did or didn't do, he was very much mistaken.

'That is not what I meant.' He stepped even closer, his height looming over her. She looked up at him, holding his gaze, challenging him. His musky scent, with hints of exotic places, tormented her senses and she fought hard to remain composed and in control.

'What did you mean, Kazim?' In a bid to divert her mind, she pulled the wig from her head and shook out her glossy black hair, thankful to be able to discard the false blonde locks for the evening. What she hadn't expected was his reaction.

His eyes darkened further, the gold flecks of anger smouldering into bronze, melting into the depths of midnight blackness. He swallowed hard, the tanned skin of his throat catching her attention as he did so. His breathing deepened and he clenched his jaw, focusing a penetrating gaze on her.

She was trapped, utterly transfixed by the sheer masculinity of him. That raw vigour, which had snared her heart when they'd first met, left her unable to break eye contact. She couldn't even step back away from the fire which had somehow ignited between them, threatening to burn her if she dared to go nearer. But, like a moth to the flame of a candle, she felt compelled to, even knowing it would destroy her.

She blinked rapidly and took a deep breath. She couldn't allow herself to weaken, couldn't allow the attraction she'd always had for him to rule her.

He looked at her through narrowed eyes. 'You can't have forgotten the last time I saw you. You were busy taking your clothes off then too.' The words snapped like bullets from his lips, hard and accurate. 'So the fact that you work here, in this low-life hole, comes as no surprise to me.'

She wanted to close her eyes in shame at the memory. In her innocence, she'd thought she was doing the right thing on their wedding night, being something she wasn't—daring and seductive. His playboy reputation was well known and she hadn't wanted him to think her uselessly inexperienced.

'I haven't got time to argue with you and your ego.' More furious than ever, she resisted the temptation to throw the wig at him. 'Just tell me what you want, Kazim, and then leave—for good.' Those last two words rushed from her and settled around them with finality.

'What I want?' His eyes hardened so much they resembled obsidian, blackness obliterating all the gold sparks. Without mercy, they bored into her.

'Just say it,' she taunted and turned to walk away. She needed to get some clothes on, cover her body with something that would protect her from his scrutiny. 'You want a divorce.'

She threw the words over her shoulder as she pushed open the dressing room door, secure in the knowledge he wouldn't follow her, and tossed the wig onto the cluttered table, knocking over a lipstick. She let out a breath she had no idea she'd been holding, desperate to get a grip on her emotions.

The lock clicked as the key turned and she whirled round to see Kazim standing there, in the dressing room, his back to the closed door, arms folded across his chest and that ever-present air of superiority coming off him like a tsunami.

'Divorce is not an option.' His abrasive words robbed her of the ability to think, let alone speak. If he didn't want a divorce then what did he want from her? What was so important he'd not only tracked her down, but had come personally to this—what was it he'd called it— *low-life hole*?

Kazim watched the colour leach from Amber's face. Even her scantily clad body paled as the implication of his words sank in. As the only son and heir to the Sheikh of Barazbin, taking as his wife the woman selected by his father had been his duty. Just as it was now his father who had forced him to seek Amber out. But he'd never expected to find her in a place like this.

His wife, Princess Amber of Barazbin, was working as a waitress in an establishment that was little better than a strip club. He put aside the shock of just how low she'd sunk and forced his attention back to what he'd come here for.

His wife.

She turned from him and he looked more closely at her profile as she dragged her hair, shorter than it had once been, quickly into a ponytail. Her gaze was rigidly focused on her image in the mirror, as if she couldn't bear to look at him, but he was drawn to her full and very kissable lips.

She glared defiantly at him, stirring something deep within him, but giving into those carnal thoughts would not help his current situation. He needed her back in Barazbin, living as his wife, and he had every intention of achieving that.

'Divorce is the only option as far as I'm concerned. Your rejection as good as told me that, Kazim. You left me in no doubt that our marriage had ended before it had begun.' Her stern voice, laced with a husky note, rattled his senses.

She cleaned her face of make-up, carrying on as if he wasn't even there, and when she looked at him again she appeared younger than her twenty-three years, but very much a woman. A beautiful woman who almost distracted him from his purpose. And he couldn't allow that.

'You must have heard of my father's failing health.' He unfolded his arms and clenched his hands at his sides, the anger when mentioning his father as fierce as ever. Regret tore through him like a sandstorm.

'I've made it my business not to keep up with happenings in Barazbin.' Her words were short and sharp, increasing his anger. 'There's no need. I'm never going back there.'

He had not expected this—a challenging woman, one who ignited his anger and stirred his blood in equal measures. She was no longer the amenable bride he'd turned his back on. She was a woman who possessed every charm necessary to weave a spell on a man. But she was his wife nonetheless. A wife he had every intention of returning to Barazbin with.

'If you don't mind, Kazim, I'd like to change.' She shot him a haughty look, her delicate brows rising in challenge.

'I have no objection to you putting on some clothes, no.' If she covered herself he might be able to think more clearly. It might stop the wild heat that raced in his blood—something which was becoming harder to ignore by the second.

Her hands rested on her hips and, just as he had been moments before, he was mesmerised by her long legs, showcased spectacularly by the corset-style costume. Her narrow waist, highlighted by those ridiculous pink feathers.

'What I meant was that you should leave.' Irritation rang in her voice as she glared across the small room at him.

And give her a chance to run out on him, just as she'd done the morning after their wedding? He hadn't even decided what would happen next, how they'd go about living their lives separately. She'd just left and he couldn't risk her doing that again. His father had made that plain.

'When I leave, it will be with you or not at all and, as I have no wish to be seen on the streets of Paris with a stripper, I suggest you get dressed.' He stepped into the room, drawn to her, until her sharp words halted him, making him stand firm once more.

'I am not a stripper.' Shock resonated in her voice and she stepped back from him, as if burnt by his words.

'From what I recall, you are very, how shall I say, rehearsed at taking your clothes off.' He remembered again their wedding night, the teasing way she'd removed the silk that had covered her body, tossing it carelessly around the suite. 'Isn't that what you did on our wedding night?'

Her lips pursed and she took in a deep breath. The shock and anger of finding out she worked in such a place still roared in his blood. Her claim that nobody knew her real identity was certainly true. It had taken several months to track her down.

'I am a *waitress*.' She emphasised the last word vehemently.

'That may be so, but I saw what was going on out there when I came in.'

'What you saw, Kazim, was dancing.' Her hands pressed heavily against her hips, anger rolling off her in furious waves.

He frowned and stifled a smile of triumph as he saw a flush of irritation cross her face. He didn't say anything more, just raised his brows in question.

'Have it your way.' She shrugged her shoulders and turned her back to him. 'But if you want me to change so that I look less like a stripper, at least make yourself useful and undo me.'

At first he could only look at her bare shoulders, her dusky skin so tantalising that he wanted to trail his fingertips across her back. He looked at the seemingly endless hooks which fastened the corset tightly around her body and scrunched his fingers hard into the palms of his hands. What was she trying to do to him?

'It will be much quicker if you do it for me and, as you've locked the door, nobody else is going to come in and help me any time soon.'

She stood resolutely with her back to him, impatience in every word she said.

He sighed, beginning to open the fastenings, his fingers brushing against the warmth of her skin. He gritted his teeth hard against the onslaught of desire that flooded him, angry she could have such an effect on him.

Kazim thought back to their wedding night. Amber had surprised him that night when he'd told her to return to her family. She hadn't dissolved into female hysteria and had shown strength she'd kept hidden from him during their short engagement—strength he now saw again.

'What's wrong with your father?' Her soft voice rushed him back from the past and he baulked against painful memories as the last of the fastenings on the corset opened, revealing the enticing smoothness of her back. She distracted him from everything at that moment—his reason for being here and the trauma of his childhood.

He couldn't take his eyes from her as she clutched the costume against her and hurried behind a screen. Seconds later, the garish outfit was slung over the top of the screen and his mind raced into overdrive, colliding with images from their one night together. It was almost as if she was deliberately distracting him—again.

What had she been saying? Quickly he gathered his thoughts. 'He is frail and weak.' *On the outside, at least.* He kept the words calm, devoid of emotion, because he didn't want to allow himself to think. Not even for a moment. He closed his eyes, forcing down the memories he would have to carry for the rest of his life.

'I'm so sorry.' Her soft words rescued him from thinking as she came out from behind the screen, dressed in jeans, long boots and a chunky knitted jumper. She didn't look anything like the woman he'd married. Nobody would ever know who she was—a princess on the run. No wonder she had managed to blend in with those around her in this unsavoury part of Paris so successfully.

'That is why you must come back to Barazbin. I am the sole heir.' He resisted the urge to tell her that their marriage must provide heirs for the country. That was a given fact.

She shook her head. 'No, Kazim, that's never going to happen.'

He sighed impatiently. 'I am concerned for our people. There is trouble within our lands and our nomadic tribes are paying a high price. Your absence has brought my ability to rule into doubt. You *will* come back with me.' He watched as she pulled on her coat and picked up her bag. It was as if she wasn't listening. 'Amber. Do you understand what I'm saying?'

Irritation surged through Amber, instantly replacing the softer emotion she'd felt for Kazim as he'd told her about his father. 'Oh, I understand, Kazim.' She reached behind the formidable figure of her husband and unlocked the door, wondering why she hadn't thought to do that earlier and throw him out. But one look at his face, as their eyes collided, told her why.

There was something between them, something undeniable. Irritation verged on anger at his demands and she pulled hard at the door. 'You think you can send me away and order me back at your whim.'

With lightning speed Kazim turned, pressed his hand against the door, his height towering over her. She looked at the long tanned fingers of his hand and shook her head. 'Let me out, Kazim, or I will call security.'

'Security? In a place like this?' An icy edge had crept into his voice and she looked up into eyes so cold, so devoid of emotion, she had to stifle a gasp. 'I would be interested to see how they handle it, a man and his wife wanting to talk.'

'I don't feel like your wife, Kazim. It has been

ten months since we married and this is the first time I have seen you.' Did he really think he could play that card on her?

All the hurt and anger she'd kept inside her since that night bubbled up, giving her the confidence to face the man who had broken her heart and shattered her foolish dreams.

'We married out of duty, Amber, never forget that.' His calm voice was full of authority, his expression harsh and forbidding. 'And now my duty is to return to Barazbin—with you.'

She laughed, a nervous laugh, but a laugh nonetheless. For a moment, confusion raced across his handsome face and her laughter died. She didn't know that much about the man she'd married, but she did know he commanded authority and didn't expect anyone to challenge his decisions. As the son of the Sheikh of Barazbin, Kazim didn't lack any of the power his father possessed. He was powerful, both in business and position, and right now she was left in no doubt of just how much.

'I haven't got time to discuss this now,' she said, looking boldly up at him. 'I need to go home before the manager realises I'm still here and…' Her words faltered for a moment and, like a hawk, Kazim pounced on it.

'And what, Amber?' He leant his shoulder casually against the door, folded his arms and looked down at her, making her feel as if she were a petulant child that had just been scolded.

Amber thought of all the times the manager had tried to force her to dance, insisting her talents were wasted as a waitress. He'd taken every opportunity he could to try and push her into dancing and if she lingered here any longer he would think she had changed her mind. Kazim's brooding presence wouldn't be any kind of defence because she had no intention of admitting to anyone he was her husband.

'He will think I want more work,' she said, forcing firmness into her voice. 'So, if you will allow me past, I need to go.'

For a moment Kazim's gaze held hers, questioning and searching. Her stomach filled with small butterflies and she was compelled, as if under an ancient spell, to hold his gaze, to look into the inky depths.

If only she hadn't tried so hard on her wedding night. She'd only done it because she didn't want Kazim to think she was totally inexperienced.

Snap out of it, she reprimanded herself as she glimpsed once again the handsome prince she'd worshipped from afar for too many years. *This is the man who rejected you, the man who ruined your whole life.*

'I will come with you.' He pushed his body

away from the door and unfolded his arms to stand looking down at her, a smile tugging at the corners of his mouth. Not a real smile—it didn't reach his eyes. It was the smile of a man in control. Complete control.

'There's no need.' She grabbed the handle and pulled the door open, about to step into the corridor, when another dancer barged through the door from the club, the heavy beat of the music becoming louder again for a moment. The dancer rushed towards the dressing room, instantly stopping when she spotted Kazim.

'I will escort you home,' he whispered softly near Amber's ear and then stepped close behind her like a territorial lion. She saw the shock on the other woman's face—shock that quickly changed to a gushing smile when Kazim turned on his charm, directing his next words at the dancer. 'We shall leave you in peace.'

Amber fumed inside. How dare he insinuate he was going home with her? They'd never leave her alone now. She could hear their questions already. Spurred on by anger, she marched the opposite way along the corridor, out through the back door of the club and into the narrow streets of Paris.

It was cool for summer and a keen wind rushed along the streets. She pulled her collar up and began the short walk to her flat, hoping

with every step that Kazim wouldn't follow. His
footsteps behind her told her that hope was useless. She accepted the fact he'd found her and
would now know where she lived, but she could
not and would not go back to Barazbin. She was
needed here.

'My car is around the corner; there is no need
to walk.' He pulled her to a stop as his hand took
hold of her arm, the contact sending a rush of
heat through her.

'So is my flat,' she fired back at him, a sense
of satisfaction settling over her as he glanced
briefly up and down the street.

'You live here, in this street?' The streetlights
cast a golden glow over his skin and his eyes
seemed darker than she'd ever seen them. The
disdain in his voice was so obvious she wanted
to laugh at him, the irrational urge bubbling up
like a fountain.

'Is there something wrong with this street?'
She wished she was brave enough to ask him
why he truly wanted her to return to Barazbin,
but she wasn't. It would mean hearing again his
blatant dismissal of her as a woman.

'The only thing wrong with this street is that
it isn't in Barazbin.' His words shot at her so fast
she almost unbalanced as she stepped back. His
hand gripped tighter still onto her arm, drawing
curious stares from a couple passing by.

'You sent me away, Kazim.' She pulled her arm free. 'I assumed if I heard from you again it would be for a divorce.'

The sound of someone approaching made him turn and look, but when he returned his attention to her his face was full of fury. 'We can't talk here. We are drawing too much attention.'

'There isn't anything to talk about. I'm not going anywhere with you. I'm needed here and, right now, I'm late so, if you'll excuse me…'

Without waiting for his response, Amber walked away, her heels tapping out her frustration and echoing down the street. She glanced at her watch and her anxiety levels rose even further. She really was late and she'd promised her flatmate she'd be finishing early this evening.

She turned the corner and glanced back to find Kazim catching up with her. 'Oh, no, please,' she sighed out the words. A persistent desert prince was not something she wanted to deal with tonight, but she might as well get it over and done with. All she needed to do was convince him that a divorce was the best option—for both of them.

Amber pulled the key from her bag and stopped by the old wooden door, the green paint somewhat weathered. Next to her, Kazim swore—a growly sound of native words she hadn't heard for a long time. It reminded her of her family and briefly she missed them, until she remembered how they'd treated her. How they'd turned their backs on her, sending her away to distant relations in England after Kazim had rejected her, insisting it was to avoid a scandal.

'Couldn't you find a better place to live than this?' Abhorrence filled his voice and she turned to look up at him as he cursed again under his breath. 'What did you do with all the money I gave you if you didn't use it for a decent place to live?'

'What I did with the money you used to pay me off, get me out of your life, is no concern of yours.' She machine gunned the words at him, more angry than ever as the pain of his outright rejection of her as his wife surfaced. He'd ruined her life. In one night he'd made her nothing.

She wasn't about to tell him she hadn't received any money from him, or anything else for that matter. If he thought she'd wasted it, so much the better. It could only help her to prove how they needed to end the marriage. 'It's none of your business what I spend my money on.'

'It was to support you, so that you could live in a manner befitting your position as Princess of Barazbin.'

She hurried into the hallway of the large Parisian town house, with its hints of a glorious past, and rushed up the stairs. As she reached her front door she turned to see him taking the stairs two at a time. 'Since you seem intent on following me into my home, you'll have to give me a minute. I need to check on Claude and pay the babysitter.'

'Who is Claude?' Cold fury sounded in his voice as he looked at her with hard eyes.

'My flatmate's son,' she said as she put the key in the door. 'Once I have done that I'll give you a few minutes—before you go.'

Kazim's mind raced. It was as if he'd stepped into an unreal world from the moment he'd entered that damn club. The anger he'd felt knowing his wife worked in such an establishment had made it almost impossible to go in. He'd stood on the threshold calming himself before he'd entered. His wife worked and lived in the most rundown area he'd ever seen in Europe.

Just as he had done outside the club, he stopped, desperately hanging onto his control, as Amber turned the key in the door and entered one of the smallest flats he'd ever seen. Did he want to go in? Did he want to bring this woman back into his life—a princess whose tiara was well and truly tarnished? A woman who seemed adept at keeping secrets from him?

She turned to him, holding one slender finger

to her lips in a plea of silence, and something twisted deep inside him. What, he didn't know, but it was almost primal and totally unexpected.

Despite everything that had happened, he wanted her as his wife and as a woman. She was his, and he was going to claim her back. Whatever the cost.

CHAPTER TWO

THE SMALL FLAT became invaded with the essence of Kazim, that raw power which had attracted Amber from the moment they'd met. His presence seeped into every corner and Amber shivered. The flat was too confined to contain him. He belonged to the desert with its vast wildness. Nothing or nobody would ever completely tame him. The realisation hurtled at her. They were worlds apart.

The babysitter, totally in awe of Kazim, hurriedly left and a heavy silence filled the air as he looked at Amber, his eyes sharp and soul-piercing. Amber had to face what was coming; it was the only way to be able to put the past behind her. If she didn't, she'd never move on in life, never be able to find that elusive dream of happiness and love elsewhere.

'Do your family know you are living like this?' The door had barely clicked closed behind the babysitter before his words were out, sharp and insistent.

His anger seemed to make him grow taller, his shoulders broader, much more intimidating. An impatient sigh escaped him as his mouth set in a stern line and he folded his arms across his chest.

She would not let his regal show of power unnerve her, and met his gaze for a second or two. It felt like an eternity as his eyes bored into hers.

'Quietly—Claude's sleeping,' Amber said softly in an attempt to defuse the increasing tension and walked into the kitchen, dropping her bag in the usual place. She turned and looked up into Kazim's face, wild and thunderous as he stood in the doorway, realising she hadn't acknowledged his question, let alone answered it.

'I'm not asking about the child.' His words came out in a gravelly attempt at a whisper, the heady scent of male wrapping itself around her.

'Where I live has nothing to do with you, Kazim.' She stood firm, refusing to be intimidated.

He took another step closer and she couldn't help but move back against the kitchen cupboards, the small room totally dominated by him. He was too close and she couldn't think straight, not when his intoxicating maleness invaded every pore in her body, making her want something she could never have. Something she should never have allowed herself to imagine.

'Keep your voice down,' she whispered harshly, hoping it would hide the colour creeping across her face. Would he guess her thoughts, know just how much he affected her?

'How can you have turned your back so easily on your family? Your country?' Anger sparked in Kazim's eyes and she wanted to look away, but couldn't. She had to be strong, had to face him head-on.

'You dare to ask that when you sent me away just hours after we were married?' Indignation rose up, fuelling her anger until it matched his. Had he any idea how humiliating it had been to go back to her parents because he didn't want her?

She pushed aside those raw emotions, unable to deal with them right now. He'd dismissed her as a wife and as a woman and she should hate him for that. She did, but she couldn't stem the sizzle of awareness that raced between them, stronger now than it had ever been.

'But to live here, in a place like this, with a woman and her child? I'm assuming your friend is not married.' The disgust on his face mirrored that which she'd seen on her wedding night as she'd tried to be anything but a naïve virgin.

'You assume right,' she said, glaring up at him.

Amber thought of little Claude, always with a

sunny smile despite his continued health problems. He'd captured her heart from the moment she had first met him, much like Kazim had done, but she couldn't allow her thoughts to wander there again. She had to stay completely focused on this moment and the brooding and overpowering presence of the man she'd married out of duty to her family.

She couldn't drag her gaze away as Kazim looked at his watch, his jacket sleeve pulling up to reveal a tanned wrist, dusted with dark hair. Amber's stomach fluttered and she practically had to force herself to think clearly. After all he'd done, all he'd said on their wedding day, she couldn't believe he was still able to give her butterflies and make her head light.

She'd never wanted any man the way she wanted Kazim, and that had to change if she was going to be able to move on in life. But while Kazim still held her foolish heart she'd never be able to look at another man and feel this sizzle of hot desire.

'Where does the child's mother work? At this hour?' He raised a brow at her and she wished he would step back, give her space to think, because having him so close was making that impossible right now. If she closed her eyes for just a moment, she was sure his musky aftershave alone would transport her back to the desert. A place she'd turned her back on for good.

'At the club.' Amber knew it was nearly time for Annie to come home and part of her wanted that to happen right now, but another, more rebellious, side wanted to keep that moment at bay for as long as possible. But if Annie did come home, at least then she could go somewhere else to talk with this man, somewhere bigger, a place that didn't heighten his power and command so dramatically.

'She is a stripper?' His accent deepened and the hard angles of his face furrowed into a scowl as once more he jumped to conclusions.

'They are dancers, Kazim; they dance, they don't strip.' She flew instantly to Annie's defence, using the exact same words her manager had used as he'd tried to lure her to dance, insisting her pay would increase substantially.

'So your little stunt on our wedding night was a dance?' His voice had deepened and turned husky, making her stomach flutter uncontrollably as he reminded her once again of that night. He stepped closer, invading her mind, her body and her soul.

She looked up at him and saw that the black depths of his eyes had changed, swirling with something new, something undefinable. She was mesmerised, unable to think at all, stunned into silence.

'Do you remember?' he asked, his voice softer than she'd ever heard it as he lifted her chin, forcing her to look into his eyes. She became swallowed up by the fire she now saw there. 'You danced then.'

This couldn't be happening. She didn't want it to happen; she couldn't let it happen. What she needed was to be free of him and letting him touch her, letting him look into her eyes with such potent need, eroded every last bit of determination she had.

'I did not dance or strip,' she flung at him, infuriated by the way her body reacted to his touch. But at the same time she didn't want him to stop. Attack, she decided, was the best form of defence. 'I was doing what I thought was right, what I thought a man of your reputation would want.'

'A man of my reputation?' He said the words slowly and suspiciously, as if he couldn't believe she was using such a thing against him.

'I was sure an innocent woman was not what you were used to.' She looked right into the depths of his eyes, boldly challenging him to deny what she said. 'I was certain you wouldn't have wanted me—a virgin bride—and I was right.'

She saw his face harden, saw his jaw clench.

She was right—he hadn't wanted her, an innocent bride, but neither had he wanted her when she'd hidden behind her attempt at seduction.

'Or is it that I just didn't fit into your world?' She threw the question at him. 'Is it because I have English blood in my veins?'

His silence spoke volumes, but she ploughed on, trying to ignore the intensity in his eyes.

'My mother may be English but she has adopted the ways of the desert to the extent that she wanted our marriage as much as our fathers did.'

Kazim looked into Amber's beautiful face, imagining how her soft skin would feel on his fingertips, and wondered how she could think that, let alone say it. For the entire duration of his wedding day he'd been consumed by need for his young bride; her innocence had been so beguiling. It was as if she'd cast a spell on him, but a spell he had no intention of slipping under. He didn't dare.

He'd fought her magic so well that, by the time they were alone, he was once more the totally in control desert prince who took only what he needed. It wasn't until she'd dropped her act of purity, throwing herself at him, flaunting her body so brazenly that he knew he couldn't live a lie, and that the rumours of her time in boarding school must have been true.

What if he was like his father? Anger had surfaced, threatening to break out like a captured wild animal. Alarm bells had gone off. She'd already roused his passion with her dance and it had mixed potently with anger at her deception.

The marriage had been a mistake—one he was certain his father was well aware of and had forced him into, testing his loyalty to family and country. All he'd been able to think of was that he didn't want to be responsible for breaking such spirit. He didn't want to replicate what he'd witnessed as a young boy.

In a desperate attempt to make Amber see reason, Kazim's words had been harsher than he'd intended. He had used her alluring dance and attempts to seduce him as an excuse. To make her believe that he was sending her back to her family because she wasn't the meek and biddable bride he'd thought she had been.

Amber hadn't shown any shock as he'd told her their duty was done, that she must return to her homeland. In fact she hadn't shown any emotion at all, had shut him out. Had she been relieved she didn't have to stay in Barazbin?

If he closed his eyes long enough, he could still picture her, seductively removing the silk that had clung so temptingly to her body, as if it was something she was used to doing. Didn't her present job confirm that?

He'd been unable to move, unable to stop her, telling himself that her actions would help. They had both needed the marriage as much as the other and consummation wasn't optional. But still he hadn't been able to touch her, let alone make her his. He was the son of a cruel, hard sheikh and he had no intention of crushing her beautiful spirit as savagely as his mother's had been. It was why he would never allow himself to love or be loved.

'You most definitely danced,' Kazim said, his voice deep and husky with the memory of that night, but not completely caught up in the moment. 'Piece by piece, you removed the silk that covered your body.'

'It was not a dance, Kazim, merely a necessary smokescreen. I tried to be something I wasn't. I tried to tempt you.' She looked up into his eyes, her almond-shaped ones searching his, and he had the urge to touch her face, feel her skin beneath his fingertips. 'But you made it clear that the idea of such an act repulsed you.'

'Repulsed me?' He lowered his hand before temptation got the better of him, and looked into her eyes. How on earth could she think that? Hanging onto his control that night had been the hardest thing he'd ever done, but necessary. He'd wanted her so much but was stunned to realise the palace gossips had been right. A virgin bride would never know how to act so enticingly. 'I never expected such a show of... knowledge.'

'I made one mistake, Kazim, and because of that you didn't want me. You just wanted me for who I was, for the benefits to your kingdom the marriage brought.' Her eyes held an accusing light as she narrowed them slightly. 'Were you secretly glad you could banish me from your life?'

If only she knew. He'd wanted her with a carnal need that had beat like a drum inside him, demanding satisfaction, but he'd restrained himself. To protect her.

He could still see clearly the image of her slender body, almost naked, as she'd tossed the silks of her wedding veils across the floor. Transfixed, he'd watched while she'd pulled too hard at the final piece, the silk tearing. She'd thrown it aside, a teasing look on her face as their eyes met. He'd demanded she stop with a harshness he was unaccustomed to and, from the wounded look on her face, neither was she. He'd sounded cruel and hard, exactly like his father.

She had disappeared into the bathroom. When she came out, her glorious body wrapped in a towelling robe, his passion, aroused by her dance, hadn't needed any further invitation. Again he'd resisted, using his anger as a shield. Whatever the reason for her behaviour, he couldn't take advantage of her. If they came together as man and wife, it would be because they both wanted to provide Barazbin with future heirs. Passion and desire didn't have any place in their marriage.

As dawn had crept across the sky he'd abandoned the idea of sleeping in the chair and stood beside the bed, watching the woman he'd married, one he'd wanted but couldn't have. He'd savoured the soft sighs she'd made in her sleep, the sweetness of her face, because they would never be his. He'd done his duty. He'd married her, but he couldn't stay with a woman who deceived him, hid her past. Not when she could provoke him so easily. For her sake, she must leave.

'The validity of our marriage was never questioned, even after you left,' he said, dragging his mind back. He stepped away from her before he gave into the urge to kiss her. He'd never tasted her lips, never felt them burn with passion beneath his and right now it was all he could think about. 'What you did that night, your discarded clothes, it worked. Nobody has ever challenged the marriage.'

'I wish it hadn't.' She tossed the words at him as she moved out of the kitchen, her arm brushing against his in the small space. In the dim light of the hallway he watched her take off her coat and hang it up, drawn to the way the denim of her jeans clung to her long legs. 'I will admit what I did. Explain exactly what happened then you can annul the marriage.'

He shook his head and followed her into the hallway. 'It's too late for that, Amber.' He couldn't allow her to bring their marriage into question. Ever.

She turned to look at him, her face partly shadowed by the dim light in the hallway but her words defiantly clear. 'I can't go back to Barazbin. I don't *want* to. I'm needed here.'

Everything had changed so much and he was to blame. He was the only heir to the throne and his father was sick. For the sake of his country he didn't have time to end one marriage and make another. He needed to be seen with his wife—the woman his people had witnessed him marry, the one they'd welcomed warmly. To annul the marriage now would make his people doubt him. If he couldn't hold together a marriage, how could he rule a country?

'People may not believe your claim if your *profession* is discovered. Do you really want that scandal exposed? Your father's people, as

well as mine, would turn their backs on you.'
He let the words sink in, watched as her lovely
eyes widened in shock. 'The only thing that can
save your reputation now is me.'

'You're despicable,' she whispered, every syl-
lable full of contempt. With barely contained
fury in every step, she walked a few paces to
another door, opened it and peered into the near
darkness.

As she slipped into the darkened room he remembered the child and irrational anger consumed him once more. Why was she living here,
sharing a cramped flat with a single mother who
worked as a stripper? Was she trying to blacken
her reputation beyond redemption?

Kazim stood and composed himself, steeling
himself against the irrational anger that raged
inside. He clenched his fists and closed his eyes,
willing control to return.

Moments later, composure seeped through
him and, unable to help himself, he pushed the
door open a little wider to reveal Amber tuck-
ing a young boy into a tiny bed. The child mur-
mured in his sleep and she ruffled his blond hair
before pressing a kiss to his forehead. From the
little he knew of children, he guessed the boy
to be around two.

When Amber looked up her eyes met Kazim's
and something akin to embarrassment briefly

washed over him at having witnessed the tender moment. He'd intruded. The shock on her face told him that, but he wasn't going to let her off so lightly. He stood and looked back at her, his stomach turning against the thought of what could have been if he'd succumbed to his desire, if they'd had a child as a result of their wedding night. He didn't want to be a father, to expose a child to the same upset he'd known, but his position in life meant fatherhood was an obligation. He had to have a child—an heir to Barazbin.

In the dim light of the room he couldn't see her expression clearly. 'If you don't mind...' Amber whispered so softly he almost missed the words.

In silent agreement he stepped back a pace. The child's bedroom was not the place for such discussions so he left, pulling the door closed again, and walked back to the depressing and claustrophobic kitchen, all sorts of questions racing through his mind.

Moments later, she stood in the doorway, hands on hips, her body poised as if ready for battle. 'Give me one good reason why I should care what your people say of me, why I should care if my reputation is ruined, as you so nicely put it?' Fighting spirit resounded in her voice but he refused to rise to the bait.

'Your family.'

* * *

Pain lanced through Amber as she looked at Kazim's questioning face. 'I haven't seen my family since the day after we got married.'

The day you rejected me as if I were an unwanted parcel.

When her father had sent her away she'd begged her mother to help her, but her mother, committed to the ways of the desert, had turned her back on her, just as she had the Western world from which she'd come. To Amber's mother, arranged marriages were now normal and acceptable. It was as if she was trying to erase her English ancestry and, along with it, the scrapes her daughter, Amber, had got into at boarding school.

Lost in thought, Kazim's next words hurtled her back to reality, dragging her back from the hurt of her parents' rejection and disappointment.

'So you turned your back on your family as well as your heritage, to come to Paris and work in a club.' He folded his arms across his chest, his dark eyes glaring accusingly at her, and she thought he was going to taunt her again, almost force her to admit to being a stripper instead of a waitress.

Did he really think she'd willingly left everyone behind?

She deflected the hurt, just as she had done on their wedding day, allowing all that pain to turn to anger. If he wanted to think badly of her then it could only help her cause to be free. He might be the man she'd loved from first sight, the man she'd dreamed of raising a family with, but he was also the man who would never love her. It was time she accepted that and moved on.

'Where I work and what I do there is irrelevant,' she snapped at him, wishing she'd never let him into the flat. But this needed finishing; she needed to be free of him. 'What is important is that here, with the two people who mean more to me than anyone else, I am needed and wanted.'

The only other person who'd ever made her feel needed and wanted was her grandmother, and Amber had missed her terribly since she'd passed away. So, since Annie and little Claude had stumbled into her life, Amber was happy for the first time in many years. They more than made up for the fact that the only job she could get without proof of identity was in the club.

'You are needed in Barazbin.' Like an arrow, his reply shot across the room, the words wounding deeply.

'Needed, maybe,' she said in a soft teasing voice, her head to one side as she shrugged her shoulders, trying hard to appear indifferent. 'But not wanted, Kazim. Not by you.'

'My father is ill,' he said, his face paling and his eyes becoming haunted. For a moment she felt his pain, wanted to reach out to him, but she couldn't. To show such weakness would be fatal. 'It is my duty to secure the future of Barazbin.'

'That still doesn't have to include me, not when we haven't seen each other since our wedding day. You even admitted my reputation would be brought into question. Your duty doesn't have to include me.' She clung to the hope that he would see she was far from suitable to be his princess, especially now. But his decisive stance warned her that such hope was futile.

'You are my wife.' He stepped towards her, the words coming out slowly and firmly, the air around her becoming thick and heavy as he towered over her, making breathing normally difficult. 'And you will come back with me.'

Amber sighed. When was he going to get it? To understand he couldn't just dismiss her from his life then drag her back into it when it suited him? 'That little boy needs me.' She pointed towards the bedroom door where Claude lay sleeping.

'And why is it so important that you are here,

when you are not his mother?' He sounded angry now, as if his patience had slipped away to nothing. 'If I didn't know better, I would question exactly whose child it is.'

How could he even think such a thing? She had never been intimate with a man. All she'd done was heed her mother's warning of Kazim's reputation with women and had tried to be something she wasn't. A seductress. The disgust she'd seen on Kazim's face plagued her still.

Amber groaned heavily, tired of talking in circles, and repeated herself. 'I'm staying here, Kazim, where I'm needed and wanted.'

'Why?' Suspicion laced the word and she knew he wouldn't give up until he knew the truth.

'Claude needs an operation. A life-changing operation, one that will mean he can walk and grow up as normally as possible.' As much as she tried, she couldn't keep the passion from her voice. Meeting Claude and Annie had been life-saving for her and she wanted to give something back to the two people in the world who'd stood by her when nobody else had. If they hadn't come into her life when they did, she would have been homeless.

He stood tall and firm, his handsome face furrowed into a frown as he digested the information. 'That is no excuse at all. Why do you have to stay?'

'Have you no idea of real life, Kazim?' Now she was angry. 'Annie is a single mother. One who works hard to provide for her son, and yes, she works as a dancer in the club. Do you know why? Because Claude needs to go to America as soon as possible for operations that will cost more than Annie can ever dream of earning in a regular job.'

'So why are you involved?' he snapped angrily. 'What about her family? The child's father?'

Amber remembered the day Annie had told her that she and Claude were alone in the world. All of Amber's own pain and misery at Kazim and her parents' rejection paled into nothing. Helping Annie had become her focus in life.

'They disowned her.' She stood fiercely, looking into his eyes. 'And I know exactly what that feels like.'

'Your family disowned you?' Shock resonated in his deep voice and he came closer to her—too close.

'After you sent me away, yes, I was disgraced in my family's eyes, forced to leave Quarazmir to avoid the scandal. I was disowned. Just as Annie was.' It was that one connection that had created a very strong bond between the two of them. 'Because of that, I intend to do all I can to help her.'

Amber watched as Kazim took a deep breath in through his nose and could see the anger bubbling inside him. His lips pressed together in a firm line as he exhaled and she felt a dart of satisfaction rush through her. Finally, he was realising the implications of what he'd done.

A key turning in the front door drew their attention and he looked at her in question. Seconds later, Annie breezed in, her usual buoyant self. 'Oh, what a night,' she whispered then stopped as she saw Kazim, her eyes wide with shock.

'Annie, this is Kazim. I was just telling him about Claude.' Amber saw the usual sadness wash over her friend's face and hated that she'd had to mention it.

'I'll just go and check on him and leave you to it. If you want me to, that is.' Annie looked from Kazim to Amber, a worried expression on her face.

Amber's heart warmed at the genuine concern her friend was showing. It seemed that Kazim didn't completely intimidate her and that, if need be, she'd stand by her friend.

'I'm fine, thanks, Annie,' she whispered and gave her a reassuring smile, all the while feeling Kazim's eyes on her.

'If you need anything, though,' Annie said softly before she slipped into Claude's room and they were alone again.

Amber felt drained, too tired to deal with Kazim, too tired to talk any more about something she had no intention of doing. 'You need to go now.'

'Not until I have your word that you will come back to Barazbin with me.'

She shook her head slowly, drawing on new reserves of determination. 'No, Kazim, I can't; this is where I belong.'

Amber opened the front door of the flat and stood back, her chin held high, waiting for Kazim to leave. She had nothing more to say. Their marriage was over.

He walked towards her and stopped. In hushed tones, he threw everything into turmoil. 'The child will have the operations he needs; I will see to that.'

Kazim's words rushed at her and she could hardly take them in. Claude was going to get the help he needed—from Kazim?

Amber's breath shuddered in and she clutched the door for support. 'You mean you will help us?' Hope soared inside her. Claude was going to be able to walk.

'On one condition.'

She frowned, her eyes searching his handsome face. 'Condition?'

'That you return to Barazbin with me.'

She shook her head, small frantic movements of disbelief. 'No.' How could he ask that of her?

Kazim stepped so close that he towered over her, dominating the very air she breathed. 'He will have all the operations he needs as quickly as possible and I will set him and his mother up in a home, wherever she wants to be. They will be secure and safe whilst the child grows up.'

'But...' She couldn't even put a sentence together. To be given everything she wanted and to have all she'd fled from forced on her at the same time was too much.

Finally she could breathe and think. Would he be so ruthless? 'What if I say no?'

'Then I will walk away from here. We will have nothing more to do with each other—apart from a divorce.' There wasn't a second's pause before he answered. He was as mercenary as ever.

'That's blackmail.' Her fingertips touched her lips as she looked at him, totally unable to believe he could be so callous, so unfeeling.

'No, Amber. It's just a way of getting what we both want.'

'You're unbelievable.' She fought hard against the urge to pummel her fists on his chest as frustration erupted like a volcano inside her.

How could he put her in such a position? Claude would be well and Annie would have a home, but it wasn't just Kazim who would give them that. It was her too.

'The decision is yours, Amber. I will return at first light and I expect you to be ready to leave.'

CHAPTER THREE

As the sky lightened over Paris, Amber quietly closed the door of the flat. She'd left a note for Annie, explaining she had to go away for a while but saying nothing about Kazim's promise or, rather, his blackmail. She hadn't known what else to tell her. How did you explain a husband you'd never mentioned, let alone that you were a princess and far from an ordinary girl?

As if conjured up by her thoughts, what could only be Kazim's sleek black car purred to a stop in the narrow street. She swallowed down the guilt of running out on Annie, which mixed with the nerves of what she'd agreed to do. Was she really about to go back to Barazbin?

She took a deep breath of early morning air and blew out softly, trying to still her nerves. She was going back, but it would only be for a while; of that she was certain. Just until Claude was well enough to return home, then she would too.

Amber looked at the car and what it represented—her return to a life she'd thought she'd turned her back on. Ever since the day she'd left, she'd thought that if she ever heard from Kazim again it would be to arrange their divorce. Although secretly she'd wished he would turn up and whisk her back to his kingdom with declarations of true love.

The thought that he'd turn into a ruthless blackmailer hadn't entered into the equation at all. She stood on the steps and looked down at the car, its darkened windows preventing prying eyes, and for a moment she had to fight the urge to run away, as far and as fast as she could from the hand that fate had dealt her.

'Good morning, Princess.' The driver got out and walked around the car to her, his greeting rasping her already jittery nerves. Where was Kazim? Was he so sure she'd go back with him that he hadn't even considered it necessary to fetch her personally?

For a moment she wanted to bolt back inside the flat. If he couldn't be bothered to greet her himself why was she even thinking of going with him? Did he assume he could just pack her up like a parcel and send her back to the desert?

The driver took her bag and opened the back door of the car. Apprehension skittered over her as she stepped into the spacious interior. But it was already occupied. A startled gasp escaped her before she had a chance of regaining composure as Kazim sat, full of regal command, watching her.

Calm, completely sure of himself and devilishly handsome, he sat and watched her as she froze, unable to sit or turn back. She could see the question in his eyes and wondered if he sensed the turmoil racing through her at top speed. Warily, she sat opposite him, not daring to get too close to the commanding presence that radiated from him and was sapping her strength.

Nerves mixed with anxiety, making her irrationally angry. He hadn't bothered to get out of the car, much less speak to her. She shot him a glare. 'You could at least say good morning.'

He smiled. A slow sexy smile that deepened his eyes to the colour of the midnight sky. He was far too sure of himself. 'If it makes you feel better, I will. Good morning, Amber.' His voice sounded deeper, more intense than she had ever noticed before. 'It is, however, not long since we parted.'

She refused to rise further to the bait and focused instead on the streets of Paris, the daily life she'd found so entertaining beginning around them. As the car moved silently, like a predator stealing her away, she glanced up at the magnificent buildings. Then the chic cafés that she'd always promised herself she'd visit passed before her, teasing her with all she hadn't yet done.

It didn't seem possible that this man had managed to turn her life upside down again. Worse still was the fact that she'd given him all the ammunition he'd needed, by telling him about Claude. He wouldn't have had any kind of lever if she'd said nothing. She should have just refused to go back with him. Insisted on a divorce.

'Not long enough,' she said quickly, her tone flippant. 'I just wish our next meeting had been for the purpose it should have been for—to arrange a divorce.' She turned to look at his face and tried not to pay any attention to the way her body reacted to being so close to him. Those childish dreams of passion and happy endings needed to be stamped out once and for all—and quickly.

'Things have changed.' He leant forward in the seat, coming too close to her, serving only to increase her irritation. His heady aftershave, potent within the confines of the car, caused her heartbeat to accelerate rapidly. She couldn't allow him to affect her like this, to turn her insides to molten lava with just a look. She had to maintain control.

'It's you who came to find me, Kazim. It's *you*

who needs *me*.' She injected a steely edge into
her voice, wondering why she'd ever agreed to
his demands—but instantly reminded herself
of Claude. This could be his only chance to get
the treatment he needed. So, for Claude, she
would go. She would protect her foolish heart
and keep her distance from Kazim. It was the
only option she could see right now.

He sat back, the movement drawing her from
her thoughts, and she watched as he reached inside his jacket pocket for his phone. What was
wrong with him? He couldn't even give her his
full attention.

'No, Amber, it is you who needs me. You
want funds for the child's operation and, deep
down, you must want to please your family, to
build bridges. You need this marriage as much
as I do.'

She clenched her teeth, biting back the retort.
How could he think she wanted to please her
family after they'd disowned her? There was
no going back; they'd made that quite clear. 'I
don't have a family, thanks to you.'

He looked at her and a question sparked in
his eyes but he said nothing, his silence goading
her, making her press home her point.

'You saw to that when you sent me back to
them. They were so horrified and ashamed that
you'd turned your back on me, they sent me to

England.' But England hadn't quite been the punishment intended. She'd met distant relations of her grandmother's and there had gained the strength to move to Paris, a city that had always entranced her.

It still hurt like hell to think of her father's proud face, barely able to conceal his disappointment. Her marriage, he'd told her, hadn't achieved anything but disgrace as far as he was concerned. If her husband had turned her away after one night, her father had raged, then he too had no option but to send her away.

Amber looked at the passing streets, the impressive Eiffel Tower as it rose skywards above the city. She hadn't even made it there, let alone the galleries and museums. But she hadn't expected to be leaving so soon.

'They shouldn't have done that.' Kazim finally spoke, his voice velvety-smooth yet hard-edged, and she reluctantly dragged her gaze from the beautiful city. 'Your father got what he wanted out of our union. His lands are now very prosperous.'

She shook her head. 'You don't understand, Kazim.'

'What is there to understand?' His expression hardened as he looked at her before returning his attention to his phone. Seconds later he spoke into the phone in his native tongue and, like a chant, it wound its way around her, tugging at her memories. It took her back to the days when she'd been happy, the long lazy days of childhood spent in her father's homeland, Quarazmir, to a time when all had been right in her world. At least until she'd been sent to boarding school in England to enable her to learn more of her English heritage, something her father had insisted upon and her mother had fought hard against.

Amber pushed those thoughts aside as Kazim finished his call, slipped the phone back inside his jacket pocket and looked at her. 'The jet is ready and waiting. We shall be there in little more than an hour.'

'An hour? I thought we were going to Barazbin.' Confusion pushed aside her daydreams of times long since passed, sharply bringing the present into focus.

'I am on my way to England. I have business to conclude before returning to Barazbin.'

Shock ricocheted through her like a pinball. He hadn't come to Paris especially for her. He'd just stopped off on his journey as if she was nothing more than an irritating loose end that needed tying up. Anger quickly followed the shock and she clenched her fingers tightly in her lap, her nails biting into her palms.

'You should have told me. I could have made

better plans for leaving.' *Or not left at all*. Then she remembered Claude and what he stood to gain from her deal with this devil. Guilt tore through her once again. She was doing this for Claude and Annie, not for herself and never for Kazim. As soon as she could, she would leave Barazbin and her marriage behind.

'What plans would they have been? To slip away, assume a new identity and take on another job in an equally unsavoury establishment?' Although his deep voice was courteous there was an underlying patronising kick in it.

She blushed. He'd guessed her thoughts but she kept her voice light, trying to provoke a reaction from him, to shake his rigid composure. 'Would you rather I had told everyone who I was?'

'No.' His voice was brusque as she sat forward again. 'But be warned, Amber. If this episode in your life gets out and threatens all I'm trying to achieve in Barazbin, you will pay dearly.'

'Now we are getting to the bottom of it all.' She smiled sarcastically at him. 'Just what is it you are trying to do—apart from blow my life to pieces again? Why exactly am I, the woman you married and turned your back on in one night, so necessary?'

Just when she thought she was about to unravel the mystery of Kazim's sudden intrusion into her life, the car stopped. The private jet looming above them brought reality hurtling at her.

She was about to leave with Kazim—a man who had dismissed her from his life so coldly. She had no idea when she would return to Paris, but one thing she was sure of was that she would not be staying in Barazbin long.

'We're here,' Kazim said, grateful for their timely arrival at the airport. He'd nearly let things slip, nearly told her she was not only of paramount importance to his succession to the throne, but crucial in a deal he was making—a deal to secure peace to his people, a deal very important to him. It was his duty to return to Barazbin with her. A duty he intended to fulfil, whatever obstacles he had to remove.

He'd always wanted to help the nomadic tribes, previously his father's venture. Now it was time for Kazim to step aside from his successful oil company and take up the position he'd been born to. Duty called and that call was becoming increasingly more insistent.

In an effort to forget a life he'd been forced to forgo, he focused his attention on Amber, watched as she all but physically rooted herself to the seat, her full lips parting, drawing his gaze, and his control wavered. She'd thrown herself at him on their wedding night and he'd turned his back on her. He'd had his reasons—good reasons. But now he couldn't ignore what he'd felt that night, stirrings of passion so strong it still simmered in his blood. He wanted her.

Was that so wrong? For a man to want his wife?

He leant further forward, closing the distance between them, surprising himself as much as her, as his lips claimed hers. A dizzying sensation hurtled around his body as he met no resistance from her, her lips moving beneath his. After a second she stilled as if she was about to pull away then her lips parted against his, encouraging him. She tasted of mint, so clean and vibrant it infused his body, making him want much more than a kiss.

The polite cough of the driver and the cool air rushing into the car dampened the desire flooding his body and he moved abruptly away. Her lovely face was flushed beneath her dusky complexion, her eyes burnished bronze and her lips plump and extremely kissable.

His body stiffened. As did his resolve to achieve what he'd set out to do. Reclaim his wife. It was more than time to claim his bride, make her his.

'You are my wife, Amber, and it is past time

you started being just that.' The harshness of his voice had echoes of his father, but he couldn't dwell on that now. Not when hot desire raced around him in a way he'd never experienced before.

'No, I can't.' Her eyes were wide with shock, her cheeks lightly flushed, fuelling his desire even more.

'I will not accept that. You belong to me and it's time I claimed what is mine.' Even to his ears his words sounded barbaric, like something uttered by a sheikh of many years ago—or his bullying father. He'd never wanted to be either but as soon as his lips had touched hers he'd lost all reason, all ability to think rationally. Wildness raced in his blood, driving him on.

'Please, Kazim, I can't be your wife,' she begged, her eyes beseeching him. 'You can't just whisk me back to Barazbin.'

'We're not there yet.' A gust of wind all but snatched his words away as he got out of the car, tossing them around the airfield, and he saw a frown of confusion furrow her brow.

'Why did I have to come now?' Amber got out of the car, the wind pressing her blouse against her, and he savoured her slender figure until she glared at him. She stepped closer to him, her chin lifted in defiance and, although her height didn't quite match his, she was still tall for a woman. 'I'm not a wayward pet that needs bringing to heel.'

'This way,' Kazim said, touching her arm and guiding her towards the plane, determined not to rise to her provocation. At his side, she kept pace with his strides and it felt strangely right to be walking with her, as if they were matched and meant to be so.

'We will stay in London this evening. Tomorrow, we will attend a polo match where I am due to meet with several other rulers. Once my business is concluded we will return to Barazbin.'

He climbed the steps into the small private jet, turning as he entered it. 'From the small amount of luggage you have, I'm assuming you don't have evening wear or anything suitable for a polo weekend.'

'Weekend? This is getting worse by the minute, Kazim. Why can't I just travel back to Barazbin with you?' Her eyes were wide as she stood on the threshold of the jet, looking like a startled animal. A flicker of guilt pulled at him but he couldn't afford to heed it now, not when so much was at stake. If emotional force was needed to keep her at his side then so be it.

'Do you really need to ask?' He pushed aside all notions of guilt, needing to remain focused.

'Yes, as a matter of fact, I do.' Indignation made her stand tall and he met her gaze, seeing the challenge in her eyes.

'You could refuse to go.' She would have every right to do so. He knew that, just as he knew how he'd handled things on their wedding day would be enough to make any woman turn and run. But she hadn't, because last night he'd seized the one thing that meant something to her and used it to his full advantage. She'd made it all surprisingly easy for him.

'As long as you keep your side of the bargain and send Claude to the States, I will go with you. For a time, at least.' Her eyes hardened and deepened to mahogany as she looked at him, defiantly laying down a challenge. He held her gaze and something zipped between them—something more than just attraction and desire. Again, he ignored it—for now.

'The child will have his medical treatment; you have my word. I will send the one person I trust above all others to ensure that.' The flight attendant halted any further discussion on the subject as she showed them to their seats and carried out the necessary safety checks in the cabin. He sat and relief rushed over him as Amber did too, but she didn't look at him, pretending instead to be engrossed in a magazine.

Amber wanted to get up and run out of the plane. She watched as the flight attendant closed the door, its heavy clunk ominously final. Was it final? Was she leaving to go back to Barazbin for good? No—she shook her head in silent denial—she couldn't do that.

As the jet soared up into the sky she gripped the seat, keeping her attention focused directly ahead of her. Could Kazim really appear out of nowhere and blackmail her to go back and be his wife—forever? She didn't think she had the strength to resist him for long. His kiss just now had proved that. She'd wanted to push against him, but instead had yielded. What would have happened if the driver hadn't opened the door at that moment?

The plane levelled off and she turned to look at him, finding he was watching her intently. 'How long am I expected to be in Barazbin?' She was amazed at the calm tone of her voice and, judging by his expression, so was he.

'That is a strange question when you are my wife.' He treated her to one of his most charming smiles, the kind that had robbed her of her heart within seconds of seeing him for the first time.

She'd been young and naïve then, swept up in the romance of being engaged to such a handsome man. She'd known of him long before she'd met him and had fallen in love with what she now knew was the fantasy conjured up by her imagination.

'For almost a year, Kazim, we have led completely separate lives. I am your wife in name only, nothing more.' *Because you refused me, turned me away in disgust.* The words were on the tip of her tongue and she pressed her lips firmly together to prevent them from leaving. He must never know how humiliated she'd been when he'd rejected her. A man legendary for his prowess as a lover, her mother had warned, would not be expecting a simpering girl. Heeding that warning had been her one mistake and one which ended her marriage before it had begun.

'I have been busy with many problems since our wedding. I hope now all those issues can finally be resolved. My father's ill health worsened the situation, forcing me to return to the palace. On our return, all will be well.' His words rushed her back to the present faster than the jet was flying. She mustn't dwell on that night. She had to be as strong as he now was; it was her only defence.

'Our return?'

'Yes, Amber. You are Princess of Barazbin and you have a duty to your people, just as I do. Your return is expected in the current circumstances.' Had she missed something when her mind had been back in the past? Had he told her just why he was demanding her return?

'What circumstances?' She heard the slight tremor in her voice and hated herself for it.

'As I explained last night, my father is ill. He is a weakening man and, despite whatever else I think of him, he is a good ruler. He wants to secure the future for his people. A future both you and I are duty-bound to play a part in.'

'I am not returning to Barazbin with you out of any sense of loyalty or duty to your people...'

His words cut across hers. 'They are your people too.'

She took a deep breath, composed herself and spoke with as much regal dignity as possible. 'I am returning because you have blackmailed me, using a young boy who is in desperate need of help. That is the only reason I am going anywhere with you, Kazim. Don't ever forget that.'

Not because I am still in love with you.

He rubbed his finger and thumb over his jawline as he took in her words, the shadow of stubble rasping, snagging her attention. His eyes narrowed with suspicion, irritation clear in his voice as he leant towards her. 'It is not blackmail. It is a mutually beneficial arrangement. One we will both gain from.'

How could he possibly believe that, when he'd plainly stated he would walk away from her and from Claude if she didn't agree to return to Barazbin with him?

She looked at him, aware of the hum of the jet's engine, taking her on the first part of her journey back to his country, a place she didn't want to go. And she was going because he held all the cards, wielded all the power.

'It's blackmail, Kazim. And you know it.'

CHAPTER FOUR

FROM THE HOTEL window Amber studied the view of London, desperate to do anything other than face Kazim as he shut the door of their suite. The flight from Paris had been short, but she was so tired, so emotionally exhausted, she might as well have flown around the world. Not a word had been exchanged since she'd accused him of blackmail. He'd read over papers until they'd touched down in London, his silence brooding and ominous.

'We have a dinner engagement this evening. I trust you have something befitting your position to wear.'

His voice held an irascible tone and she turned from the window and stared at him.

He looked tired. Something tightened inside her, just as it had done that first moment she'd seen him on their wedding day. His raw masculinity then had robbed her of the ability to think clearly and now she wondered if it had all gone wrong from that moment. Had she fallen in love with the man she wanted him to be rather than the man he was?

'If you had told me I would need evening wear I could have packed something for the occasion.' Precisely what that would have been, she didn't know. Nothing in her wardrobe would have been remotely suitable for dining out in public with a man such as Kazim. She'd left the glamour of a desert princess behind to take on a normal life. And she'd achieved that, proved to herself she could survive—until Kazim's arrival had sent the first blocks of her new life tumbling down. 'I'll stay here. You go.'

She turned her back on him and focused again on the view of Knightsbridge bathed in sunshine. Every time she looked at Kazim, a tingle of awareness slipped down her spine and when his gaze met hers that tingle intensified, just as it had done from the moment they had first met.

As Amber continued to study the view Kazim's silence almost frazzled the air but, as far as she was concerned, it was settled. She wasn't going with him this evening. Determined that she wouldn't be swayed from this decision, she folded her arms across her chest, ignoring the urge to turn and look at him again. But it was too much and finally she gave into the temptation. When she turned round it was to find him looking at her, his eyes narrowed, his stance regal and loaded with authority.

He was the epitome of power, his shoulders broad enough to carry the burdens his position in life had given him, but, as a man, his tall figure held an air of isolation. Did he ever let people close?

'Are you determined to cause trouble, Amber?' Command rang in every word he spoke. 'You are my wife. My princess and, as such, you will go where I go—at least until we return to Barazbin.'

That told her enough. As soon as he returned to his homeland she would be forced into the role of dutiful wife and once again be surplus to requirements, but she had to go if she wanted Claude to get the treatment he needed. Even though Annie didn't yet know what chance her son had, Amber couldn't deny him. Once the treatment was over she'd leave, return to Paris and Annie's unwavering friendship. Why stay with a man who didn't even like her, let alone love her? One who'd shredded her heart as if it were nothing more than waste paper.

'Well, you'll just have to go alone tonight because even if I did have something *befitting my position* to wear, I would rather stay here.' She knew she shouldn't be provoking him, but she couldn't help it. Just because he was a desert prince didn't mean he could order her around, especially as he'd been constantly reminding her she was *his* princess.

Her heart rate accelerated and butterflies took flight in her stomach as he walked across the room. His strikingly handsome face was marred by a thunderous expression as he came close to her. 'We made a deal, yet already you think you can assert authority over me.'

She stood her ground despite wanting to slip past him. 'I have not yet received any kind of indication that you have honoured your side of the *deal*, as you call it.'

'Is my word not enough for you?' he said as he walked away again, giving her the impression of an animal trapped in captivity, stalking the perimeter of its reduced territory.

She looked at his broad shoulders, tight and firmly set. He had exploded into her life again, opening up wounds which had only just begun to heal, and the only way she could tolerate it was to know that he would keep his promise of helping Claude.

'No, it isn't,' she snapped, the rush of humiliation sweeping away rational thought. He'd married her, rejected and abandoned her. 'Why should I trust you at all when you detest me so much you couldn't stand to be near me? You couldn't get me out of your life fast enough.'

She bit back her grief and anger, wanting to be as far away from him as possible. Just being near him muddled her mind. Suddenly it was all too much and she rushed past him, grabbed her handbag and headed for the door as fast as she could. She couldn't stay in this room a moment longer with him. Her emotions were in turmoil. Emotions she'd thought she had well and truly under control were now running riot inside her.

She still had feelings for him, despite all he'd done. Feelings which meant she couldn't risk staying a moment longer with him in the suite, even with its capacious luxury.

'Where are you going?' His deep voice rang with command, but she didn't stop.

'Shopping. Anything to keep His Supreme Highness happy.'

'Sarcasm doesn't become you, Amber,' he said as he crossed the room, joining her at the door.

Her heart sank. Couldn't she go out alone now? Was this an example of what her life in Barazbin would be like? A return to the restrictions of bodyguards and servants. 'I'm quite capable of going shopping on my own.' She tossed the words at him and forced a smile.

'You can't just wander the streets of London without security or an escort. You're a princess.' He marched alongside her as they made their way to the lift.

'How dare you?' She rounded on him. 'I've been wandering the streets of Paris for the last few months, no thanks to you. I'm sure I can manage to go out alone and buy a dress in London.'

'Don't be so dramatic. You make it sound like you were destitute, when the reality was very different.' He turned as the lift doors opened, walking in without a backward glance, obviously intent on being her escort and security.

More infuriated than she'd ever been, she marched in after him. 'What do you mean: "the reality was very different"?' she asked as the lift enclosed them, wishing he wouldn't keep alluding to such things. If he'd thought she would approach him after that night and ask for financial support he didn't know her at all.

An uneasy feeling settled over her, as if he was waiting for her to trip up. He obviously didn't believe a word she said.

'You are a princess, and you should be living like one—no matter where that is.' His gaze held hers as he folded his arms across his chest and nonchalantly leaned against the polished lift wall, as if having such discussions in a lift were part of everyday life.

Shocked to the core, she could only stand and look at him, but his changing expression showed he was fast losing patience. He talked as if he'd given her vast sums of money, as if such an act had appeased the guilt of his rejection. Last night she'd pushed aside those suggestions that she'd been given money without much thought, but now it niggled in her mind.

Now wasn't the time to ask questions. He obviously thought she was trying to get as much money from him as possible. Why disabuse him of that opinion when it might just be what she needed? If he thought that was what she was doing, then getting him to agree to a divorce would be much easier, especially since she'd finally accepted the truth, despite how she felt about him—she needed to be completely free of him.

'Obviously your idea of how a princess lives is different to mine,' she taunted him, pleased when he drew in a sharp breath. Let him think she'd spent all his money. She didn't want it and she didn't want him. The important thing was to be able to make Claude well. That was all that mattered right now and she'd do well to remember that when her heart hammered as soon as he came close.

'At least we both know where we stand now.' His voice was harsh and he looked away from her, giving her the opportunity to study him. The wild ruggedness she had fallen for when she'd first met him wasn't so apparent now, as if abandoning the desert sands to rule his country was slowly taming him.

The lift doors opened onto the busy hotel lobby and she almost ran out, still desperate to put as much distance between them as possible. Everything about him was messing with her emotions. 'I'm not exactly going to run out on you. A young boy's health is now dependent on me going to Barazbin—and on you keeping your word.'

Kazim studied her for a moment and she watched a muscle flicker as he tensed his jaw, his lips pressed into a thin line of annoyance. She raised her brow at him, sending him a challenge despite knowing she shouldn't. Just what was it about him that made her act so— irrationally?

'Do not argue with me, Amber.' His firm words irritated her and she glared at him. 'I *am* coming with you.'

She sighed in resignation, which earned her a questioning look. Determined not to show him just how much he was getting to her on every level, she waltzed out of the hotel. Within seconds, just as he'd done in Paris, he fell into step beside her. She scanned the boutiques of the affluent street, knowing they would be too far out of her price range. She was certainly in the wrong part of London for her current budget.

'Kazim,' she said, stopping in the street so suddenly other pedestrians would have collided with her if he hadn't pulled her close. Flustered, she looked up into his eyes, as dark as ever, but, instead of the usual hard and passionless depths, they blazed with something so intense it echoed deep inside her. As if, with that one look, he was claiming her as his.

'What is it now?' A smile teased at the edges of his lips and her heart jumped then raced erratically, his change of mood confusing her, disarming her.

She swallowed hard, not wanting to admit anything to him but she had no choice. 'I can't afford to shop here.'

'We'll go to the next one then,' he said without taking his eyes from her face. Heat was spreading from his touch and the world around them stopped, blurred into oblivion, ceasing to exist. The hum of the traffic slipped away and it was just the two of them.

Mentally she shook herself, trying to clear her head, her cheeks flushed with embarrassment. 'What I mean is I can't afford anything, not from this street.'

He let go of her so abruptly she almost stumbled and the noises of the traffic rushed at her as if someone had suddenly turned the volume back up.

* * *

Kazim kept a tight rein on his temper. She certainly knew how to infuriate a man. He had no idea why he'd even decided to go with her. Shopping in any form was something he just didn't do. But he'd glimpsed a hidden part of her as she'd studied the view from the suite earlier. He'd seen vulnerability as she'd stood at the hotel window. Vulnerability he was now compelled to protect.

Of course his security team would have discreetly followed her, just as they were doing now, but she'd stirred in him an old need to protect and, along with it, bad memories from his childhood.

He took her hand and the moment of hesitation in the soft brown of her eyes almost made him waver. 'In here,' he demanded roughly, not comfortable with the direction of his thoughts as he imagined her dressed for dinner in a sexy figure-hugging dress. 'Get what you need for tonight and a further two days. I will attend to the bill.'

Her hand loosened within his as he strode into the nearest boutique. He glanced down at her; the expression on her face was so desolate, so untainted that he wanted to hold her hard against him and kiss her lips.

'Let's just go back.' She pulled on his hand,

preventing him from going into the boutique, but he held her hand firmly, sensing she'd slip away into the crowded street if she got the slightest chance.

'Go back?' He knew his tone was harsh, but exasperation mixed with heady desire rushed around him mercilessly. He let her hand go, pushing open the door of the boutique and leaving her little option but to follow.

Glamorous assistants rushed forward and instantly his control returned as he told them what was required, watching as they took over, guiding Amber towards the dressing rooms of the boutique. She looked back at him, her beautiful face almost frozen with horror.

He turned his back on her, unable to deal with the need to protect her from hurt and harm that just being with her ignited. It was as if he was a young boy again, protecting his mother from his father's wrath, boldly standing between, glaring at his father. He sighed and, with arms folded across his body, he stared broodingly out at the street, wondering just how everything had suddenly become so complicated.

He'd come on a mission to reclaim his wife but, as he surveyed the passing traffic, he begrudgingly accepted why it was so important. He wanted to prove, once and for all, to his father that he was worthy of his time, his respect.

Failure wasn't an option, even if it was what his father had cruelly taunted him with, despite his weakened state of health.

Kazim had to succeed, he had to return with Amber and take up his role as heir, but he hadn't expected to want Amber so intensely, nor had he expected the desire that hummed through him just thinking of her. But, worse, he hadn't anticipated she'd open up his past, bringing back the heartache from childhood and making him think and rationalise things he'd rather forget.

But something else wasn't right—ever since the first moment they'd spoken, almost everything had come back to money. He'd sent her father money that would support her, but still it seemed it hadn't been enough. Just what had she spent it all on?

He pondered the question. Why live in such an appalling flat when he'd been more than generous? Was she really as broke as she'd just alluded to? Something didn't quite make sense.

Kazim turned his attention back to Amber, who was now watching as a seemingly endless bundle of bags were packed. He settled the bill and asked for the purchases to be delivered to the hotel without passing any comment. A discussion of what she'd done with the money could wait until later.

'Let's go,' he said quietly, an unmistakable

firmness in his voice. He was all too aware of her standing close to him. He could feel the heat of her body as if he stood in the middle of the desert beneath the sun's unrelenting heat. 'We have a few matters to sort out, Amber.'

'Only your impossible attitude.' She glared up at him as the heated words left her lips and he realised the assistant was tactfully looking down, studying the final bag just a little too much.

'We can discuss that too if it makes you happy, but not here.' He kept his voice light, wanting to avoid a public discussion. He hoped the assistant would be discreet. The last thing he needed right now was extra attention from the press. Headlines about his marriage would not help anyone.

He looked at Amber and she dropped her gaze, her face looking so young and inexperienced he fought against the urge to kiss her, as he had earlier. Not just a brush of the lips, but a kiss full of fire and passion. Maybe he should just do it and get it out of his system instead of wondering how she'd taste, how her lips would feel against his. That gentle brush of lips in the car hadn't been nearly enough. All it had done was ignite the flame that had simmered since they'd first met.

Before he had time to say anything further

she all but flounced out. He couldn't believe how out of his depth he felt with her, just as he had done on their wedding night. The reasons had been different but the feelings the same. She brought out a passionate streak in him, something no other woman had done, and he didn't like it. Not one bit.

Amber couldn't remember walking back to the hotel, but now she was once again within the confines of their luxury suite, wondering how Kazim managed to irritate her so much. He stood watching her, his presence dominating and consuming every breath of air. What was he waiting for her to explain? What did he want her to say now?

The need to speak was taken away as a knock at the door broke the tension between them. She watched as an endless array of bags was delivered. Had she really bought that much? He must think her a shallow spendthrift. But it was what she'd wanted him to think, so why did it matter now?

'I trust you are happy with your purchases,' Kazim said, his mood changing as he closed the door. She looked at him, taken aback as a glimmer of humour lightened his eyes and tugged at his lips, melting her heart with incredible speed.

'Yes, thank you,' she said softly, wanting to

defuse whatever it was that zipped between them, because retaliation certainly hadn't helped so far. 'There was no need for all of this, though; it cost a fortune.'

'You are married to the Prince of Barazbin.' He glared at her, that moment of humour gone, as if he thought she'd made a judgement on him. 'There are certain standards to maintain. That is why I have been more than generous already.'

She frowned. Was he now going to bring his offer of treatment for Claude into all this? 'And I'm grateful.' She was. To think that Claude could finally get the treatment he needed and Annie would be able to give up a job she hated to look after her son. That reason and that alone was why she was here having this discussion in the first place.

Before she had time to think further, Kazim crossed the room and stood perilously close to her. Just as it had done when he'd held her on the street, her heart raced wildly and she slipped once again under his spell. She swallowed hard against skittering nerves which sprang to life, intensifying his touch. How had she ever thought she could remain immune to him? Just his voice was enough, but to have him this close was far too much.

Amber looked up into his eyes, which searched her face as if looking for answers, or trying to convey something to her. She dropped her gaze, suddenly shy. Gently, his fingers lifted her chin, forcing her to look up at him again. Her breath caught in her throat as he slowly lowered his head, his lips brushing over hers, making her eyelids flutter and close.

She swayed towards him, wanting more, needing more. This was the only man she'd ever wanted. One she'd stayed true to, despite his hurtful rejection of her on their wedding night. She blushed as she remembered that night. It had been her complete inexperience that had made her all but throw herself at him. She hadn't wanted him to think she couldn't even kiss a man. She'd flirted, flaunting herself, and had tried to kiss him.

She could still feel the shock that had iced her blood as he'd pushed her away, a look of repulsion on his handsome face. She'd been so determined not to show her hurt she'd continued the act of bravado, anything but admit failure.

His fingers, warm under her chin, now melted that ice and she allowed herself to be just what she was—innocent and inexperienced. Because right at this moment she couldn't be anything else.

Kazim pulled away and her eyes opened. Nervously she looked up at him. The swirling desire in his eyes was not what she'd expected to see. His fingers still held her chin and the pad of his thumb moved to rub lightly over her lips, prolonging the tingle his kiss had started. She dragged in a ragged breath, wishing he would kiss her again, but not daring to move, not wanting to risk his rejection once more.

'You should get changed.' His voice was husky and a shiver slipped down her spine, but still he held her there. Then, briskly, he moved back, broke the spell, startling her. 'I have a call to make, so I shall leave you in peace to get ready.'

Amber blinked against the shock of what had just happened. She touched her lips, her hands shaking. Was it possible that he didn't hate her as much as she'd thought, that the gentle loving touch of his lips meant something more? Hope sprang to life and with a tentative smile she gathered up the bags and headed for one of the bedrooms to shower and change.

A short while later, nerves skittered through her once again. She studied her reflection in the mirror. It had been so long since she'd worn such lovely clothes she'd almost forgotten how it felt.

The black dress moulded to her body, the sweetheart neckline scooping perhaps a little too low, but the shoes that had been insisted upon in the boutique were gorgeous. Strappy black sandals encrusted with so much sparkle every small move made them glitter—expensively.

Was this a little too much for dinner? She was about to slip them off and go for her usual choice of plain heels when an impatient knock startled her.

'It is time to go, Amber.'

Shyly she opened the door, watching his handsome face for a reaction. Had she chosen well or overdone it? Her skin heated as his eyes slid slowly downwards—it was almost as if he was caressing her with their dark depths. She held her breath. When his gaze moved back to her face the desire swirling there shocked her, setting off a chain reaction of fizzing heat hurtling through her.

'You look...' he paused, his head slightly at an angle '...exquisite.'

Unable to help herself, she let her gaze linger on his face before taking in the full impact of him dressed for dinner. The crisp whiteness of his shirt made his tanned skin more pronounced, the formal black tie suit fitted him to perfection, showcasing his strength perfectly. The Western clothes highlighted his rugged power, intensifying the rush of heat around her body.

When she looked back up at his face, he was smiling, a kind of sexy come-to-bed smile that made her heart crash inside her chest. It was like floundering at sea. She was truly out of her depth with Kazim.

'Do I measure up?' he teased and stepped back a pace, allowing for better scrutiny.

'I think you know the answer to that,' she said, aware and a little unnerved by the husky tone of her voice as she opted for bravado. 'You know it only too well.'

Despite the fact that he'd just stepped away from her, a spark of fire leapt to life between them—the same heat that had been smouldering since he'd first said her name at the club. She held his look, desperately trying to hide how unsettled she was right now.

When he laughed it shocked her; it was such a deep, rich sound. Laughter lines creased at the sides of his eyes and he looked much younger. More like the man she'd lost her heart to in Barazbin—and much less troubled.

'A very brave answer,' he said as he held out his arm to her. She looked at him a moment longer before linking her arm with his, enjoying being made to feel special. It wouldn't last long, of that she was sure. So why not make the most of it? He was, after all, the first and only man she'd given her heart to.

The sensation of walking on air had little to do with the fantastic dress and glamorous high heels she wore, but everything to do with the man on whose arm she was. Beside her, he carried himself with confidence and command. Every move he made transferred to her from the light touch of her arm in his.

As they waited for the lift her heart raced and, just as she wondered if she could go out to dinner with him, the lift doors opened. Other guests spilled out and he released her arm, standing aside then waiting for her to enter the lift.

She pressed her lips together in an effort to control the dizzying effect he was having on her and allowed her eyes to close for a moment. Would he keep up this charm offensive during dinner? She certainly hoped not; every glance, every lingering look, was chipping away at her defensive wall. He'd hurt her once. He could do it again. Whatever her reason for returning to Barazbin, she could never let him know how she still felt about him.

With this in mind, she held her head high as they exited the lift, her arm once more loosely wrapped in his. They made their way towards the dining room and she sensed a ripple of silence following them, as if everyone they passed stopped to look.

She glanced at his profile. The strength and pride there left her in no doubt that he was aware of the reaction his presence was causing, just as she'd told him only moments before. A gentle hush fell on the dining room as they entered; it seemed to last an eternity, but it must have only been seconds before the maître d' came forward and showed them to their table.

The table, situated discreetly away from other diners, with candles, a single red rose, was set for two. It was beautifully romantic, but a table for lovers.

'I thought you were meeting others.' She could scarcely breathe the words out, horribly aware of the hitch in her voice.

'I changed my plans.' He dismissed the maître d' and pulled her chair out for her, his smile more beguiling than she'd seen as he invited her to sit. His charm offensive was well and truly on show.

'Why?' she asked as she took her place, all too aware of him standing right behind her chair.

He rested his hands on her shoulders and, as he leant down to her, she looked up, suddenly finding her face close to his. So close she could see clearly into the inky blackness of his eyes before her attention was drawn to his mouth as he smiled.

'It is time we got to know one another.' Each word was heavy with intent. 'Properly.'

'But...' she began before becoming too flustered to continue. Flustered as much by his nearness as the meaning in his words.

'You are my wife, Amber, and tomorrow we will be in the presence of people important to me. It would look strange, would it not, if we knew nothing of one another?'

His smile held a hint of provocation behind the charm, but at least she knew he wasn't entirely serious. He didn't really want to get to know her; it was merely a device to stop others prying too closely. A trickle of relief defused the bewildered feeling he'd caused and she reminded herself of his harsh terms, the cruel bargain he'd driven.

As he sat opposite her, his back straight and regal, she allowed a smile to spread over her lips. 'I'll be your wife in public,' she said so softly he had to lean forward to hear her. But, from the look on his face, he hadn't missed her last words or the determination in them. 'But not when we are alone.'

CHAPTER FIVE

KAZIM HAD PONDERED Amber's words as they returned to their suite. Was she really refusing to be his wife in every way? Everything they'd spoken of over the meal had been merely small talk, as if they were strangers passing the time of day. His intention had been to get to know her better, but instead she'd become more distant, more unobtainable.

Was she setting him a challenge? Or pushing him away?

'You looked very beautiful tonight,' he said as he closed the door of their suite a short while later. Would she slip further away from him now they were alone? 'Very much like a princess.'

A little shocked, he admitted to himself that he didn't want her to slip away, but maybe it was for the best. Because right now he wanted more—much more—just as he had on their wedding night. Instinct told him that to make love to her would be different from any other woman. It was not just the fact that she was his wife. It was the way he wanted her, not only with fiery blood in his veins but with something much deeper, unknown and new.

But what if the temper he'd inherited from his father surfaced as it had threatened to do on their wedding night when he'd thought of those rumours? What if behind closed doors he became the abusive bully his mother had had to put up with? He hated the fact that he looked like his father and he just couldn't take the risk that he could also be like him in other ways.

Amber turned and looked at him and, despite being only a few strides from him, the distance seemed as endless as the dunes of a desert. 'I felt like a princess.' Her voice was hardly above a whisper, but her bronze eyes watched him anxiously and a vice-like grip clutched at his chest as vulnerability showed through her armour.

He moved closer, watching her. She stood and looked at him and he took a deep breath, forcing cooling control into his body. He wanted to reach for her, to kiss her lips, her face, her body. He wanted to claim her as his own and it was that very fact that held him back.

He'd already been far too hard on her. He had no right to claim even a kiss.

'You *are* a princess,' he stated emphatically,

focusing his thoughts on other things. Just saying those words made him want to find out what had happened since she'd left the palace. 'Why did you take a job in that Parisian club, Amber?'

The colour drained from her face in seconds but she remained strong and resolute before him, indignation sparking off her like fireworks. She watched him suspiciously as he moved towards her.

'I told you, Kazim—nobody knew who I really was, not even Annie.' Her voice, though just above a whisper, was strong.

Did she really think that such assurances were enough? He needed to know more and intended to get answers. He wasn't going to be put off. He had to know. He'd been more than generous. Something wasn't right. Why had she felt the need to work in such a place and live in the terrible excuse for a flat he'd seen?

'But why there?' He narrowed his eyes suspiciously, wondering again about that rumour from her time at the English boarding school. Her display on their wedding night had already proved that attending it had corrupted her far more than anyone else knew.

'When you're not prepared to use your own identity, it's difficult to get a job, Kazim. I took whatever I could and am grateful to the women in the hostel for telling me about the job.' She raised her brows in challenge, standing tall and resolute before him as she waited for her words to sink in.

Then, with a haughty flash of her smile, she walked away from him. He watched the sexy swaying of her hips as she made her way to the bedroom, mesmerised and knocked completely off course. It was almost as if she was taunting him with her body—again. Just as she had on their wedding night, drawing his focus away from what was important with the lure of her body.

One word leapt to life in his mind. *Hostel.* Shock mingled with hot need, making any kind of reply impossible. What did she mean—hostel? He shook his head, trying to free himself of the thumping desire that rushed through him just from watching her—desire that was distracting his usual rational thoughts.

'What hostel, Amber?' Quickly he refocused his attention, not prepared to let the moment slip by. She was hiding things from him, tormenting him, and he didn't like it one bit. 'I think you'd better tell me exactly what you've done since you left Barazbin—and with whom.' The doubts he'd had about her on their wedding night surfaced again.

She sighed, but her rigid body told him she

was resigned to having this discussion. 'For a while I lived in a hostel in Paris. I didn't have help from anyone and I had nowhere to live so, princess or not, it's what I had to do.' She'd walked back from the bedroom to stand in front of him once more, apparently abandoning the idea of closing the door on him. 'Some of the girls there told me I'd easily get work at the club. I had no idea what sort of place it was.'

'But you still took the job.' He stated the obvious as he looked down into her face.

'I needed the money. Besides, I met Annie there, who offered me a place to live.' Her brown eyes looked beseechingly into his and he swallowed down hard on the guilt that threatened to drown him.

'So, Annie offered you a place to live?' He probed further, needing to know all of it. He couldn't afford to read her story one morning, splashed all over the front of a newspaper. Not now they were about to return to Barazbin.

'She was struggling, looking after Claude and working, we got on well, so it made sense. Neither of us had anyone; her parents had gone back to England, refusing to have any more to do with her.' She looked up at him innocently, her explanation as plausible as the sunrise in the morning.

Guilt tore through him. He'd done this to her. If he hadn't been so wrapped up in his problems he'd have realised sending her away wouldn't help either of them. He'd been so damned determined not to be like his father. He raked his fingers through his hair, knowing he'd been worse—much worse—than that bully.

He took Amber's hand in his and looked down at her. 'I should never have sent you away. I had a duty to you as a husband and I failed.'

'And now you are forcing me to go back, blackmailing me, using an innocent child.' Accusation hung in her every word.

'Not blackmailing, Amber, striking a deal. One which will see us both getting what we want. I thought we'd settled that argument.'

He watched as her teeth sank into her lower lip, indecision sweeping over her face. She looked the picture of innocence and he began to wonder if the rumours he'd heard of her just before they'd married really held any truth. Had they just been malicious palace gossip because of the English blood which flowed in her veins…?

'Tell me about what happened when you were in England, when you were at the boarding school.' He watched her face pale, but she lifted her chin and looked him in the eye.

It had been those rumours of her time at the

English school which had clouded his judgement on their wedding day, made him doubt his bride's innocence even before her little *dance*. Now he wondered if they had forced him to think things that might not have been true, despite the fact that he'd wanted to disregard them, but the way she'd acted had made him question his judgement.

'There is nothing to tell; not when you have already condemned me.' Her retort flew at him so fast that the pain of each word hit him hard in the chest.

'So it is not true?' He stepped closer, her stance and angry glare asserting that it wasn't, and he regretted having listened to palace gossip.

'No, for what it's worth. I was in the hotel room, not to meet with a man but to save a friend's reputation. She was the one meeting her lover, not me.' She maintained her frosty expression.

'That's it?' Her simple words didn't come anywhere near the scandal that had whispered its way into his palace within hours of their wedding.

'A friend had taken a lover, a married man, and she'd been meeting him regularly.' Amber paused to look up at him and he kept his expression impassive, hoping his silence would encourage her to continue. 'One day her lover asked her to bring a friend, saying we would all go out.'

'You went, as the friend.' It was slowly beginning to make sense. She'd been set up, sold to the highest bidder for her story.

She swallowed, lowered her eyes briefly then looked back up at him. 'This other man was a reporter on the hunt for the scandalous story that would make his career. I didn't know this and foolishly told him things I shouldn't have. My friend and I returned to school, the same way we got out, through a back window. The next day I got the letter.'

'How did you deal with that?' Kazim couldn't recall anything in the papers and surely his advisers would have mentioned the scandal during their marriage negotiations.

'My mother can be very formidable when necessary.' Amber smiled a light smile that didn't quite reach her eyes and it touched him that she'd shared it with him. If only he hadn't heard the rumour on their wedding night. His pulse leapt at the thought.

'Then I believe you.' He stepped closer, not sure if he really believed she was completely innocent, but right now he wanted to and he needed her to trust him. He needed the world to see a couple reunited and happy about it.

* * *

Amber looked into the increasingly dark depths of Kazim's eyes and her stomach tightened. 'What exactly do you want, Kazim?' she whispered so softly she wondered if she'd actually spoken.

'What I want? Right at this minute?' His voice deepened and became husky as he stepped closer to her. 'I want you.'

She dropped her chin and looked down, not trusting herself. Surely she'd misread the passion that swirled in his eyes. From what he'd said about the rumours, he'd thought she was far from a virgin on their wedding night. Had that been what had made him reject her so harshly?

Should she tell him that she'd made only one mistake? Throwing herself at him. Should she let him know the only man's lips to have touched hers since their wedding night had been his? She pressed her fingers to her lips, remembering his kiss just a short while ago.

'You didn't want me on our wedding night.' She tried to move past him but he reached out and took hold of her arm, keeping her in front of him, leaving her no option but to look up into his face.

'I didn't *want* to be married. Marriage was a duty. That was all I ever saw it as.' He kept his voice calm. 'You weren't what I was expecting. I was angry—at you and my fate.'

She gazed up at him, all the pain she'd felt that night now drowning her. She swallowed hard then took a deep breath. 'I made one mistake, Kazim, one moment of madness, and because of that you punished me, sending me away, publicly humiliating me and my family. My father still hasn't forgiven me for it.'

'None of that matters now,' he said as he brushed her hair back from her face, a gesture so full of tenderness that her breath caught in her throat. Could she really believe him? Her heart wanted to, but in her head a voice screamed caution.

She covered his hand with hers, stilled the caress that was almost loving. Just that one touch was enough to set light to her body, to ignite the slumbering heat into a wave of red-hot fire. If she didn't step away from him, break the contact, she would be engulfed and then she would want more. But wanting more from a man who had rejected her was insane.

'It matters to me, Kazim.' She pulled back from him and his hand dropped to her shoulder, preventing her from moving any further away. 'I can't go back to Barazbin. I can't be your wife, your princess, not when that one silly moment will always be between us, always causing you to look at me with disgust.'

'I don't want it to be that way, Amber.' His voice had deepened and become husky once more, raw emotion in every word. 'The truth is I want you.'

Her heart thumped loudly in her chest, an echoing pulse pumping around her body. He wanted her. It was as if, piece by piece, he was dismantling the wall of protection she'd erected around herself.

She shook her head and moved away from him, away from the temptation of his touch, his smile and his kiss. She wanted him too, so much that she could throw herself into his arms and plead for him to make her his, but such actions had caused all the pain, all the heartache she'd been living with for almost a year.

This time she would be strong, she would resist the powerful urge to be his, to allow his touch to claim her or his kisses to force her to surrender. This time she would be the innocent she was.

'No, Kazim.' She forced the words out, firmness injected into them as she tried to buy herself time so that she could gather up her wayward emotions once and for all. 'I need to know you have kept your side of the deal.'

He undid his tie, pulling it down until it hung

loosely, and then opened the top button of his shirt, revealing olive skin, dusted with hair. She knew she shouldn't look but she couldn't help herself and when she moved her gaze back to his face it was to see a satisfied smile playing sexily at the corners of his mouth.

'I'm not sure you are in a position to demand terms, Amber.' His eyes sparked with mischief, tying her stomach in knots.

She laughed softly, hardly able to believe the throaty sound came from her. 'You were the one to seek me out, Kazim, so surely that makes you the one who shouldn't be making demands.'

'Is it not you who seeks reassurance that you will get what you want?' He stepped closer to her again and she moved backwards, her legs meeting the sofa, leaving her no option but to sit down.

The softness cushioned her as she sat but instantly she wished she hadn't. He seemed so much more powerful as he towered over her. She watched, helpless to drag her eyes away, as he took off his jacket, tossing it onto a chair before sitting next to her, his arm along the back of sofa behind her head, bringing him unbearably close. So close she could smell his aftershave, the spicy scent unable to completely cover the essence of pure male.

He came even closer and she knew he wanted

to kiss her, just as she knew to allow it would be her undoing. She looked into his eyes, saw the molten bronze swirling in their depths, and knew she was lost.

His hand touched her face, caressed her cheek then pushed her hair behind her ear. The warmth of his touch as he looked down at her melted her reservations. Was it so wrong to want your husband to kiss you?

It was wrong. So very wrong and she couldn't allow it. As if the very thought provoked the action, he brushed his lips lightly over hers, teasing and tempting her. She tried to resist, tried to move away, but his hand slipped around the back of her head, keeping her lips firmly against his.

'Kazim...' She pushed her hands against his chest, shocked by the hardness beneath her palms and the way her heart skittered like a leaf blown about in the wind. 'Please, I can't. Not yet.'

Her voice echoed with appeal and as he sat back against the softness of the sofa she let out a breath of relief. The tenderness she'd thought she'd seen in his eyes moments ago was gone, replaced with granite hardness, and his lips that had set light to hers were pressed into a firm line. His mood had changed and the only reason she could see was that she hadn't responded to him, hadn't answered the primal call of her body for his.

'In that case I will leave you. I have preparations to make for tomorrow's meetings.' He stood up, towering over her, emphasising the power he had. 'Be ready to leave by ten.'

'No,' she snapped, jumping up, desperate to keep things as balanced as possible. 'I need to know about Annie and Claude. I won't go anywhere else with you until I do.'

'Now who is using blackmail?' He smiled at her, so full of self-assurance she wanted to scream.

She shook her head quickly. 'I'm merely responding to *your* blackmail, Kazim.'

'You friend's little boy will have all the help he needs. It is all in hand, exactly as I said it would be.'

'You disapprove, don't you? A stripper and a single mother shouldn't mix with a princess; is that it?' Her words were as hot as her body.

'Your words, Amber, not mine, but true.' His voice was so cool, so calm it was impossible to think this was the same man who'd just minutes ago ignited an inferno inside her.

'I will not go anywhere unless you keep your side of the deal.' Indignation made her sound petulant.

He stopped so very close she could almost

feel his breath as he lowered his head so that she thought he might kiss her again. 'I meant every word I said tonight.'

As she moved back she exhaled. At least he was going to keep his side of the bargain, but this meant she'd have to keep hers. She was trapped, being forced to do what he wanted, and she couldn't do anything about it, not if she wanted Claude to receive the treatment he needed.

He stood and looked at her, authority radiating from every pore in his magnificent body, her own protesting over what she'd denied it. She said nothing, but staying beneath his glacial gaze was as difficult as refusing his kisses.

As if he'd sensed her turmoil, her need for space, he turned and strode to the master bedroom without a backward glance. She closed her eyes in relief, thankful she'd put her things in the second, much smaller bedroom. At least tonight she would sleep alone.

Kazim shut the door on Amber and ran his fingers through his hair, the heat of desire still thumping around his body, begging for release. The first time they'd spent a night together she'd thrown herself at him and now she was pushing him away. But he knew she wanted him as much as he wanted her. He'd seen it in her eyes.

Whatever else was between them, the attraction that sizzled there wasn't going to go away and he planned to explore it.

She was his wife and he intended to claim her back—in every way.

CHAPTER SIX

THE SUN SHONE brightly as Amber watched the polo horses pounding up and down the field. This was the kind of glamour she hadn't experienced before and in her new silk sundress she felt every bit as sophisticated and elegant as the other ladies. She was acutely aware of the interest Kazim's presence was causing and the curious glances coming her way.

She slipped on her sunglasses, which offered her a place to hide, and feigned interest in the game, anything to try and avoid the tension that sliced through the air whenever Kazim spoke to those around them. His deep voice kept drawing her attention, her body painfully aware of his presence after last night.

This was the informal part of his business meeting, he'd explained as they'd arrived at the country hotel by helicopter a few hours earlier, and she was thankful that soon she could seek sanctuary in the luxury of their suite whilst he met with the other leaders in private. Being constantly near him was proving harder than she'd envisaged. In her heart she still loved him, but was it good for her to yearn after something so impossible? It hurt that he'd only looked for her out of duty and necessity and, if that hadn't been bad enough, he'd made it clear he hadn't come to Europe especially for her. She'd been nothing more than an afterthought.

'Are you not enjoying the polo?' Kazim's voice startled her and she looked up, prickles of embarrassment colouring her face and a zip of awareness shooting down her spine.

'I was thinking of Annie,' she said tentatively after his admission last night. 'I'm worried she will think news of Claude's treatment is a hoax; after all, she has no idea who you are.'

Kazim took two flutes of champagne from a passing waiter and set them on the table before sitting down opposite her, his long legs intimately close to hers, and she trembled, shocked by his nearness. 'You are correct. Annie had no idea who I was, or indeed who you were,' he said firmly. 'But that is all sorted now.'

'It is?' she questioned as she picked up her champagne in an effort to appear calm. How had Annie taken that news? Knowing Annie, she wouldn't have accepted Kazim's explanation without giving him the third degree and she smiled to herself, wondering how he'd coped with that. Maybe she should have put more in her note, explained who Kazim was, at least? 'But did you tell her about Claude's treatment?'

'I told her, exactly as I promised,' he said as he looked out at the polo match. 'Hasim, my cousin, the man I trust above all others will accompany them to America. They leave today.'

She glanced at him. 'So soon?'

Applause rippled around them and she glanced out as a goal was scored. She looked back at Kazim, who hadn't taken his eyes off the match.

'When I want something I will do whatever is necessary to make it happen.' The hidden innuendo didn't go unnoticed. He'd as good as told her last night that he wanted her. Was this his way of making it happen?

She watched as he sipped his champagne, loving the way the sun shone in his onyx hair. In fact she loved almost everything about this man. Despite all that had happened, she had done so since she'd first been introduced, the day she'd been told of their engagement by her parents. But she couldn't let him know that; she couldn't leave herself open for another rejection from him. She already knew from experience how lethally charming he could be if needed, just as he could be brutal and honest.

'Thank you.' She returned her attention to the polo match, not wanting him to see even the smallest trace of confusion on her face, because confused didn't go halfway to explaining the tumult of emotions within her.

'I always honour my promises,' he said as he moved closer to her, keeping his words just for her ears.

She turned quickly, her face suddenly so very close to his and, despite her sunglasses, she was sure he knew exactly the riot of feelings that were racing deep within her; she could see the same unrest mirrored in his eyes.

'Very commendable,' she said, adopting a light-hearted tone she was far from feeling, needing to gain control again. She had to distance herself from him, if not physically then certainly emotionally.

He leant forward, putting his empty champagne flute on the table, his gaze holding hers all the time. The simmering sexual tension that rippled between them seemed to suddenly be at the point of exploding.

'Finish your champagne,' he said, his voice seductively husky, churning her stomach and sending heat coursing through her veins.

Her breath caught in her throat and she licked her lips, which had suddenly become very dry as the intensity of desire in his eyes surfaced.

The molten bronze swirled against midnight blackness and nothing or nobody else existed. It was just the two of them.

Hesitantly, she took another sip; the bubbles fizzed in her mouth and he watched every tiny movement of her lips.

When she took the next sip heat curled around her body as if his strong arms held her against him. Then, in a slow and controlled move, he leant towards her, his lips brushing lightly over hers as if he wanted to taste the champagne on them.

She drew in a ragged breath and clutched tightly onto her almost empty flute as he drew back from her. The air around them throbbed with desire so raw she couldn't speak. She didn't want to say anything that might shatter the moment because right now she was desired and wanted by the man she loved.

Slowly and with intent, he took the champagne flute from her hand. Without taking his eyes from hers, he placed it on the table. 'Come.' The underlying sensuality in that one word was not lost on her. He took her hand, infusing her with even more heat, and stood, leaving her no option but to grab her bag and phone and go with him.

Amber was vaguely aware of heads turning and curious glances being cast their way as they left the match, but she didn't care. His hand still held hers tightly, as if he thought at any minute she would turn and run. On one level she had no idea where they were going or why, but with some kind of instinct she'd never known before—she knew.

Once inside the hotel doorway he made straight for the wide sweeping staircase that led to the first floor and the palatial suites on each wing of the grand building. She pulled off her glasses, her breath coming so fast she couldn't speak. Their bodies were communicating through the seductive waves of awareness darting between them like shooting stars.

They reached the door of their suite and he stopped and looked at her, his eyes so heavy with desire she caught her breath, biting down hard on her lower lip. He opened the door and took her hand, but she knew she would follow; she was well and truly under the spell of attraction that sparked in the air around them.

'What was that display for?' Finally she managed to get some words out. Indignation was the best form of defence, she decided, as the door to their suite closed. It was her only defence against what was happening, the only hope she had of clinging to sanity. He turned to face her. She raised her chin defiantly at him, raw desire burning in his eyes as they boldly raked over her.

'I think you know.' He swiftly crossed the room and, before she could move or say anything, he'd swept her feet from the floor and taken her in his arms. With intent and purpose he strode into the bedroom.

Her head became light and a dizzying sensation fluttered around her heart and she knew what he wanted. He wanted her. Passion boiled wildly between them and she no longer cared about what had happened in the past, or what might happen in the future. All she cared about was this moment.

He laid her gently on the bed as if she was the most precious thing ever then removed his jacket quickly, tossing it impatiently aside before covering her body with his. Instinctively she wrapped her arms around him, pulling him closer, and was rewarded with a deep guttural growl as his lips claimed hers in a hard, demanding kiss.

Her whole body sang, as if she'd waited forever for this moment. She had, and one thing was certain—this time it would happen. It was what she wanted. She wanted to be his—completely.

His hand slid down her side to her hip and she moved beneath him, giving into an instinct that rose up and engulfed her as she encouraged him to take more, to make her his.

He deepened the kiss and she spread her hands across his back, relishing the warmth of his skin through his shirt, feeling the power of his strength. Everything about that moment was as wild and untamed as she knew he was.

It was what she'd always dreamed it would be like, passionate and all consuming, not at all like she'd imagined it would have been on their wedding night. Then it would have been nothing more than a signature on a contract. This was so much more. This passion, this heated desire, it was what she wanted and, judging by his response, Kazim did too.

He broke the kiss and propped himself over her, his eyes heavy with desire. His breath came hard and fast and, unable to help herself, she slid the palms of her hands down each of his arms, savouring the strength and power of his muscles.

Her whole body was alive, tingling with desire for him. This was what she wanted but at the same time she knew it would only cause more problems, more heartache.

Kazim tried hard to rein in the maelstrom of emotions rushing around his body. Never had a woman driven him so crazy with desire that he'd all but dragged her back to his hotel room in the middle of the afternoon. But then never had a woman made him wait so long. He had, he decided, been ensconced in the desert far too long and now he had very little control left.

'If this isn't what you want...' he heard his words come out in a low growl, saw the shocked expression cross her beautiful face, but he couldn't stop them '...then I suggest you say now.'

She moved beneath him, her body pressing against his erection, and he clenched his jaw hard, hanging onto the last thread of control. She was draining the strength from him and when her hands slid down his arms he almost couldn't bear it.

Slowly she reached her hand up to his face, her palm pressing against his cheek, and he wasn't sure if she was trembling or if he was shaking with the effort of control.

'I want this, Kazim,' she whispered huskily. 'I want you.'

He pushed aside the doubts that had made him walk out on her on their wedding night. He couldn't think about them now; the raging throb of desire in his body needed quenching. It needed quenching now. He wanted her—completely.

He looked at her face, the colour creeping over

her cheeks as his hand slid down her leg until he reached the hemline of her dress. Slowly, he slid his hand underneath the silk and upwards. The soft brown of her eyes darkened, her breathing deepened and he watched in fascination as her lips parted, a soft sigh escaping them.

'Kazim,' she pleaded, her gaze fixed on his, her fingernails digging into his arms.

Just his name on her lips sent him into overdrive, unable to think of anything other than making her his. He touched the lace of her panties at her hip and pulled hard, the satisfying sound of tearing making his pulse race. He lifted himself up on one arm and quickly freed himself from the constraints of his clothes. He was too impatient to remove them all—he wanted her now.

As if in encouragement, she moved her legs either side of his and he pushed her dress up, watching her face all the time.

For a fleeting moment he wondered if he should take things more slowly, but as she moved against him, sighing softly, tormenting him with the heat of her body, he knew he couldn't.

'Kazim,' she sighed and he shook with hungry need, her husky whisper heightening his desire. Should he use contraception? The question floated on the periphery. No, she was his wife and he needed an heir. If this moment led to such an outcome it wouldn't be a hardship.

'Kazim…' She encouraged him again, her voice almost lost to pleasure, her hands pressing him against her.

He had precious little control left now; all he wanted was to be deep inside her, feel her heat surround him. She wrapped her legs around him, moving temptingly against him. He felt her wetness and couldn't hold back any longer. In one swift movement he thrust himself into her, the ecstasy of it making him cry out.

'Kazim!' Her cry of pleasure mingled with his and she lifted her hips up, meeting him, taking him deeper still, until it was as if all the stars in the desert night sky had exploded around him.

As his heart rate slowed and he regained his ability to think, he felt triumphant. She was his, but he reeled with the shock of realising that she had been a virgin, that the rumours had been nothing more than malicious gossip started by a conman on the make. Now she would always be his, no matter what.

That last thought sat uncomfortably with him. Didn't that make him as dominating as his father?

Amber dragged in harsh ragged breaths, her body shaking from the electrifying passion that had so fiercely consumed them both. She looked up at Kazim's face and it was as if the clock had turned back, as if she was once more being subjected to his scrutiny. She closed her eyes against the pain of that night, turning her head against the pillow.

She couldn't do it again. Couldn't boldly stand and take his rejection. Not now, not after what had just happened.

In one swift move his hand cupped her face, forcing her to look back at him. 'It should not have been like that.' His words were short and sharp and she bit into her bottom lip, still reeling from his wild and raw possession.

How should it have been? The question ran around her head as he brushed his lips over hers, easing the soreness her teeth had just made.

'It was your first time. I should have been gentle, more in control of myself.'

'It doesn't matter,' she whispered so quietly his eyes narrowed as he looked down at her. She could still feel the warmth of his body against her, warmth that was stirring new needs despite the words he spoke.

'It matters.' His hand left her face, the air cooling the heat on her cheek where his palm had scorched her skin. Swiftly, he lifted his body from hers and then off the bed, marching towards the bathroom. 'You deserve better than that.'

She listened as water gushed from the shower, wondering what she should now do. This was almost an exact replica of their wedding night, only this time they had made love. That night he'd strode off to the bathroom too. He'd hardly been able to hide his fury at discovering his bride was not a simpering virgin. She realised her actions had given the wrong message to him, made him think the worst of her.

She hadn't said anything, hadn't defended herself or explained why she'd done it, why she'd tried to be something she wasn't.

Suddenly feeling exposed, she pulled her dress down and, sitting up, slid her legs off the bed. She didn't know what to do now or what mood her husband would be in when he emerged from the shower.

Images rushed into her mind of his olive skin beneath the jets of water, droplets cascading down him. She closed her eyes against the thought. She might want him, desire him with a passion that could never be doused, but he didn't feel the same about her. To him, what they'd just shared was once again duty. Just as their marriage ceremony had been.

It was always duty with Kazim.

Yes, she'd married him out of love—a love born

of teenage dreams once their engagement and planned arranged marriage had been announced —but she had always been aware the untamed playboy prince everyone believed him to be took his duty very seriously.

She looked down and saw her torn and discarded panties on the floor and fire burned in her cheeks as she remembered just how wild and reckless she'd been, how totally abandoned. She'd virtually begged him. Embarrassment took over and inwardly she cringed. All she wanted to do was take off the soft silky sundress she'd bought yesterday and slip back into her usual jeans and T-shirt. She'd be safe then, able to hide once more behind her wall of defence.

Her heart pounded as she thought of what could have come of today if she hadn't been taking the Pill, for medical reasons rather than contraception. The thought of having a child, of bringing it into a family where its parents didn't love one another, was too much. She knew well enough how such a child would feel, having grown up with parents who didn't show their love to her, let alone each other.

She undid the buttons down the front of the pale blue silk dress and, despite loving its soft quality against her skin, couldn't wait to discard it. She tossed it roughly aside, kicked off her heels and yanked open the drawer to grab another pair of panties. They didn't match her bra, but that was the least of her worries now. She just needed to get dressed and quickly. The shower had stopped.

'So beautiful.' Kazim's husky voice sent goosebumps over her body as she tugged her jeans from the drawer. Holding them against herself, slowly she turned to face him.

Her mouth dried. He stood before her in nothing more than a towel slung low on his hips. A very small towel. The late afternoon sun filled the room, making his damp skin gleam, and heat gathered deep inside her as her stomach somersaulted.

He moved closer to her, his eyes, swirling with molten bronze, held hers and she couldn't move. Slowly, he reached out and tried to take the jeans from her, but her fingers were clutching them so tightly he had to tug them free. Now she had nothing to hide behind but resisted the urge to cover herself with her arms. She wouldn't let him know how uncomfortable and out of her depth she was, standing before him in just her underwear.

Her jeans dropped with a thump to the floor, but she hardly heard it over the thudding of her heart. She could smell his body, fresh from the shower, but nothing could mask the intoxicating scent of pure male. Her head spun and she kept her gaze fixed on his ever blackening eyes. To look at his naked and glorious body would be so easy, but she didn't dare. She didn't trust herself.

'This time,' he said in a thick and unsteady voice, 'will be how it should have been on our wedding night.'

Her knees weakened and she bit down hard on her lower lip, wishing she could break eye contact but at the same time not wanting to. He pushed her hair back from her face and then with both hands held either side of her head gently as his lips met hers. The kiss was soft and persuasive, teasing and tormenting her until she had no choice but to respond.

He deepened the kiss, his tongue sliding between her lips to entwine with hers, and she sighed with pleasure, her body melting and swaying towards his. Still his hands held her head, gently keeping her just where he wanted her, so that his kiss became the most erotic sensation she'd ever known, making every part of her so sensitive she could feel the heat of his body even though they weren't touching each other.

Unable to fight the instinct that seemed as natural as breathing, she traced her fingertips over his biceps, felt them flex. The growl that came from him as he kissed her harder urged her on. She slid her hands up his arms to his broad shoulders then down his back, moving her body closer to his until just a sizzle of electricity separated them.

'From the first moment I saw you, you've driven me wild.' His seductively low voice sent shivers down her spine as he broke the kiss, his hands sliding down her back, pulling her hard against his almost naked body.

The slightly coarse hair of his chest made her breasts tingle despite the white lace that still covered them. He crushed her against the hardness of his chest, her breasts pressed close to him. The ridge of his arousal, hard against her, sent shivers of anticipation spiralling around her and she dropped her head back, a sigh of pure pleasure escaping.

'And now I'm going to drive you wild,' he growled as he kissed her exposed throat until she couldn't stand it any longer and raised her head, stopping the torment.

You've driven me wild. The words floated like a dream in her head and a little spring of hope was born. He wanted her, desired her. Could there be a future for them and was it so wrong to abandon herself to the pleasure of the moment with the man she loved and always would?

Another gasp of pleasure escaped her lips as he unclasped her bra and stepped back slightly to pull the lace from her body, his eager gaze on her naked breasts, which tingled with hunger for his touch.

He lowered his head and took one firm nipple in his mouth, his tongue twisting around it, and she plunged her hands into the silky depths of his hair, closing her eyes to the sensation that raced through her. His hands slid down to the small of her back, caressing her skin and leaving a trail of fire.

'Kazim.' The whisper of his name from her lips made her heart pound wildly and she thought she wouldn't be able to stay on her feet for much longer.

His mouth left her nipple, the cool air making it tingle but, before she could move or say anything, he'd claimed the other one. The onslaught of desire continued and her hips pushed towards him.

She couldn't take any more of this. Each touch was seducing her into total surrender. Her fingers gripped his hair, currents of desire rushed through her and her knees buckled as his mastery continued.

He caught her as she slid against him, pulling her upright and holding her firmly; his lips claimed hers once more in a hard and demanding kiss, one that gave no mercy. She closed her eyes as the room spun and kissed him back.

He moved against her, forcing her to step back until she felt the bed behind her and fell back onto it, bringing him with her. His demanding kiss continued as his hand slid down her body, his breathing hard and fast. He pulled back from her and levered himself off the bed, reached down and in one swift movement pulled her panties down her legs, throwing them aside.

He stood before her as she propped herself up on her elbows, strangely comfortable with her nakedness. His black eyes swirled with molten desire, firmly focused on her. The energy that zipped between them was intense and potent, manipulating both of them. His lips lifted into a teasing smile as he pulled the towel from his hips and slung it aside, leaving him totally naked to her eager gaze.

He was magnificent, his bronzed body a work of art. Total perfection. Hungrily, she took in every detail, from an old scar on the left side of his chest to the tantalising trail of dark hair going down over his abs, drawing her gaze to his erection.

Before she could register any thoughts, let alone say any words, he'd joined her on the bed, lying at her side, propping himself up on one elbow. The heat of his body scorched into her and she turned her head to face him, wanting his kisses, needing his touch.

She touched the scar and he dragged in a deep breath. 'What happened?'

'My father...he lost his temper with my mother.' His expression hardened and her heart sank. Had she asked the wrong thing? 'I tried to protect her. But now is not the time to talk.'

She allowed her fingers to trace the scar once more and whispered softly, 'Sorry.'

He trailed his fingertips across her lips, silencing her sympathy, then down her face and throat and to the hardened peak of one nipple. He was distracting her but she couldn't help herself and writhed in pleasure as he lightly circled it before moving to the other one. She gasped as her lips sought his.

He laughed, a soft, low, sexy rumble that made her heart skitter. 'Such a beautiful body,' he said as he kissed her gently, but she could taste the underlying urgency he held firmly in check. 'And you are all mine.'

She pushed aside the words of possession, not wanting to think of anything now, only to surrender herself to this moment. 'Make me yours again,' she whispered boldly against his lips. Deep down, she knew that, whatever happened, she would always be his, that she would always love him, and right now she wanted to sample that elusive dream of love and happiness that existed only inside her.

His fingertips continued their torture as he trailed lower, circling over her stomach for a moment before moving down between her legs, to the centre of her throbbing desire. He'd barely touched her as the first wave of ecstasy broke over her body like a wild wave crashing to the shore. She moved against his touch as each wave rushed over her, threatening to drag her away.

As the last ebb of delight slid over her so did he, his hard thighs nudging her legs apart as he slowly slipped deep inside her.

'Amber—' his voice demanded her attention, but she was still floating from his touch and now the feel of him inside her was too much '—look at me.'

She opened her eyes and saw the flush of desire cross his face, saw his eyes grow heavy. His momentum increased, taking her once more to a place she'd only just discovered. Their gazes locked as she lifted her hips, moving with him, increasing the pleasure of the moment.

Harsh words she could barely recognise rushed from him as he moved harder and faster within her, taking her to the heights of ecstasy again, this time clinging to him, her fingernails deep in his back as their cries of pleasure mingled together.

She lay against the pillow, her hands absently stroking down his back as her heart rate slowed.

He rolled away from her to lie on his back and she stole a look at him, the harshness he hid behind already back on his face, and her heart sank. It had not been the loving moment for him that it had been for her.

It had been possession. Duty.

The afternoon sun had gone from the room and Kazim stirred, his body languidly replete. He was more relaxed than he'd been for many months. Was that why he'd allowed the desire that had throbbed between him and Amber to explode so spectacularly?

The second time, he'd tried to be gentle but it had been beyond him to do so. Urgency had driven him again. Memories of that altercation, the moment he'd lost all control and lashed out at his father, had been stirred by her sympathy. The scar to his skin wasn't deep, but emotionally it was still livid and raw, brought to the surface once more by Amber.

She moved against him and he wanted nothing more than to take her in his arms again, kiss her awake and make love to her for the rest of the night, but he had further meetings this evening.

He ran his fingers through his hair as the relaxed feeling he'd woken with disappeared. He should have made it clear to her exactly why her presence in Barazbin was required. He should have told her that she was not only expected to be his princess but the mother of his heir. But wasn't that why they'd married in the first place? To secure his succession and the future of Barazbin.

'What's wrong?' Her soft voice tentatively asking the question roused him from his thoughts and he looked at her lying sleepily in his bed, her lovely hair like silk spread over the pillow.

'I was just thinking about the final meetings I have this evening.' He danced around the truth, not wanting to tell her that the meetings would take place only because she was here with him, that their reconciliation was already having an effect on his country's relations with its neighbours.

'You're leaving me—again?' She smiled teasingly at him.

Even so, guilt ripped through him at the hidden rawness of the question. He'd hurt her badly before, handled it all wrong. 'For a few hours, yes, then I will be back.'

He wanted to pull her close, to kiss her and reassure her, but didn't trust his ability to control himself. Instead, he chose that moment of unguarded openness to ask what he'd wanted to ask almost a year ago. What he should have asked.

'That dance you performed on our wedding night?' He kept his tone soft and coaxing, reaching out to stroke her face.

Her eyes closed briefly but he waited.

'I made a mistake,' she said then looked at him.

'As did I.' He'd believed the rumours, which he now knew were unfounded.

'I'd hoped I could distract you… I didn't want you to think I was completely inexperienced.' She paled as she said the words and he realised he'd stopped stroking her face and that his own was set in a hard frown.

'That is why you performed that dance? So that I wouldn't think you were a virgin?' He couldn't believe what he was hearing. Surely she knew that in his culture a man prized virginity above all else when he married?

'I had been warned by my mother that you had a reputation, that you wouldn't appreciate inexperience.' Her face coloured as she explained her motives and inwardly he cursed her mother's unintentional bad advice.

He swore harshly, unable to believe what she was telling him, and she pulled back from him, physically and emotionally. 'I'm sorry.'

'It's in the past,' Amber said as she slid from the bed and disappeared into the bathroom, coming out a few moments later wrapped in a white towelling robe. 'Let's just forget it and move on. All I need to do now is return to Barazbin with you. Once you have sorted things with your father we can divorce and go back to our lives. Providing Claude has had his treatment, that is.'

He had to tell her everything.

'We can't divorce, Amber, not ever.'

Amber felt as if the floor she stood on had turned to quicksand and that she was sinking—fast. Was there no end to his ability to shock her?

She shook her head. 'That can't be right.' She'd wanted a happy ever after since she was a young girl, had dreamed of marrying a handsome prince and being loved. So far she'd only got one part of that dream.

Kazim threw back the sheets and got out of bed, not even trying to cover his naked body as he crossed the room and took clean clothes from the wardrobe. He turned to face her, his bare chest, sporting the scar, drew her attention until he spoke.

'You knew I was heir to the throne. Just as you knew our marriage was arranged to unite two kingdoms and nothing more. We should never have parted, certainly not within hours of the ceremony.' He paused and looked at her, as if letting the words sink in.

'Now your father is ill,' she whispered, more

to herself, finally understanding the implications of what he was trying to tell her.

He nodded. 'That is why you must return to Barazbin. I am the sole heir to the throne. We cannot divorce.'

'But you don't love me.' The words rushed out of her as his stern face regarded her from the other side of the room.

'Love has nothing to do with it,' he snapped and he picked out a shirt, roughly pulling it on. 'It never has and never will.'

She watched as he continued to dress, obviously preparing for his final meeting. She couldn't wait for him to go. She just wanted to be alone with her thoughts and the knowledge that she would never be free of the man she loved—a man who didn't love her.

Shock made her shiver and she sat down on the bed, hardly able to stand any longer. 'You knew this all along?'

'I am doing my duty, Amber, just as you are.'

Indignation flared to life inside her. 'By first blackmailing me and then seducing me? You even let me carry on believing I only needed to return to Barazbin for a short while.'

His handsome features clouded with anger as their eyes locked. She didn't know what to think. How had life become so complicated? *Because Kazim had come storming back into it.*

'I haven't time to discuss it now.' He strode to the door, his anger evident with every step. 'Be ready to leave for Barazbin as soon as I return. It is time to go home.'

CHAPTER SEVEN

AMBER WOKE TO new sounds as the palace came to life around her. The heat of the desert invaded her room and scents from the courtyard garden drifted in through her open window. It was a magical place but right now, just as she had been on arrival late last night, she felt immune to its beauty.

Emotionally bruised by the last few days, she just wanted to curl back up under the crisp sheets of her massive bed and stay there. She had no idea what time it was; the night flight to Barazbin had totally confused her, as had the man who'd accompanied her.

She hadn't been able to help herself and had fallen utterly under Kazim's spell. Memories of the time they'd spent making love still warmed her body. His callous dismissal before he'd left for his meeting reminded her she needed to guard her heart against him. She'd been silly to believe, even for one moment, that he really desired her. All he'd wanted was to do his duty and make her truly his wife and she'd made it easy, falling into bed with him.

She heard voices and sat up in bed, the opulence of the room startling her. High ceilings, domed and ornately painted, rose above her and the vastness of the room was broken by intricately carved marble pillars. The four-poster bed was so large and soft white tulle hung from it, draping to the floor as if the room was meant for romance. This wasn't the room she'd spent her wedding night in.

As confusion settled over her she heard Kazim's voice, unmistakable and strong. It sent a ripple of awareness cascading over her. It wasn't right that he could be so unaffected by her when she only had to hear his voice to stir all those longings.

She couldn't let those heady desires take over again. They served only to expose her emotional vulnerability—to herself and Kazim.

The tall double doors opposite the bed opened and he stood on the threshold. Nothing could have prepared her for that moment. Dressed in full white robes, he took her breath away, rendering her completely speechless. The last time she'd seen him like that it had been their wedding day.

He looked regal and totally relaxed in the palatial surroundings. A wild prince of the desert tamed, just a little, by his unwavering duty. His eyes met hers, his expression guarded, and pain lanced through her. She was back in a country she had no wish to be in, one that was painfully close to her father's country of Quarazmir and with a man who only wanted her there out of a sense of duty. But she would never let him know that and demurely clutched the sheet against her. He, on the other hand, didn't appear fazed by the situation at all.

'I trust you are rested?' The enquiry was polite, his voice resonant yet powerful; she still couldn't speak but nodded.

'Good. Your maid will help you dress then you will receive your first visitor.' He stepped into the room, his footsteps echoing on the marble floor.

He stopped by the bed and stood looking at her for a moment, his gaze locking with hers. The spark that always ignited deep within her flared into life once again. He looked as if he'd just stepped out of her wildest dreams, the ruggedness that had called to a primal part of her on their wedding day evident now Western clothes weren't able to mask it. His thick brows lifted and his face showed impatience but she could barely register what he'd just said.

'Kazim—' she finally managed to say something and briefly his face softened and he moved closer to the bed '—I must know what is happening with Annie.'

His face hardened as he stood looking down at her. She'd said completely the wrong thing, she knew that. She should have been patient and at least waited until she was up and dressed so that she could face him on an equal level. But at the same time she was here because of Annie and Claude, so wouldn't it be better to know this now, before her time as Princess Amber of Barazbin started, especially as she'd tried endlessly to phone Annie? Her only contact with her friend now seemed to be through Kazim.

'I will see that you are kept up to date with the child's progress.' With those terse words he marched from the room, the echoing retreat of his footsteps hard and furious. In just a few minutes she'd blown it, shattered any hope of actually becoming closer to Kazim. Did he let anyone close?

She hid her face in her hands and wished the last few minutes undone. Why had she said that? All she'd managed to do was remind him of the deal they'd made, the real reason she was here at all, when she should have built on those tender moments in England.

Heat flooded her as she recalled the way he'd taken her, claiming her as his. The urgency of the first time had unlocked something inside her, allowing her to throw caution aside and surrender to his mastery. The second time had been less urgent, but far more intense. For her, the moment had been loving and she'd let her love shine through, but was she now to pay for that?

Had she uttered words of love as passion had consumed them? She hoped not. Instinct told her a man like Kazim didn't want to hear such words. Her ever growing love for him was something she must keep hidden. What good would it do to love a man she couldn't stay with?

More footsteps, this time softer, drew her attention and she looked up as a young girl walked into her room, carrying the most beautiful *abaya*. At first Amber was unsure of allowing herself to be dressed. Before her marriage, it was not something she'd done but she soon gave into the ministrations of her maid, happy to be wearing such beautiful fabrics again. As a teenager she'd had the most amazing wardrobe of cool silks, but she'd quickly converted to Western clothes when she'd gone to England and now felt most comfortable in them.

A short while later she was led through to a sitting area. Another set of elegantly arched doors opened and her mother walked in. She had had no idea who the visitor was but her mother was the last person she'd expected and she greeted her cautiously, the last angry words spoken by her father, undefended by her mother, still etched lividly into her memory.

'I had not expected that you would return,' her mother said as she sat elegantly opposite her, but on the edge of her seat.

Amber watched as her mother looked around the room; nerves seemed to be getting the better of her. What had happened to the woman she'd looked up to as a child? Had her father's ambitious schemes been unkind to her also? Amber considered, for the first time, that her mother might be unhappy, that the smiles she bestowed on everyone could be a mask to hide that unhappiness.

Life had changed drastically for her mother. She'd been an English bride to a sheikh and had fallen in love with the desert and the man. She remembered her English grandmother telling her fairy stories of love and happiness, assuring her that one day she too would have her own prince. Had that been her mother's way of escape? Finding her own prince? Had it gone wrong?

Amber blinked back tears, tiredness making her too emotional to say much. She couldn't dwell on the past now; she had to look forward, to focus on doing what was necessary in Barazbin, so that as soon as she got word that Annie and

Claude were okay she could prepare to leave—
both the country and its prince—for good. She
couldn't delude herself any longer: she didn't belong here.

'You are the last person I'd have thought
would be here to welcome me home. I thought
I brought nothing but dishonour to the family.'
Finally she managed to speak, her words hard
and to the point. She wanted to let her mother
know just how hurt she'd been by their reaction
to her failed marriage. The callous dismissal of
her as a daughter had cut deep. Far deeper than
she'd realised.

Her mother stood up and walked towards her
and took her hands in an uncustomary show of
affection. 'You look well. England must have
suited you.' Her mother's words were soft and
genuine, tugging at her heartstrings and childhood memories.

'For a while, but I moved to Paris; that's
where Kazim found me.' Suddenly everything
she'd been through in the last few days was too
much and the need to confide became unbear-
able. 'He sent me away because of the school
scandal.'

Her mother tightened her hold on her hands
as if trying to infuse her with strength. 'The reporter was paid off and paid well. It will only
have been gossip within these walls. Always

remember that, Amber. Walls listen and tell all your secrets.'

Amber frowned, confused by her mother's words. 'It might have been different—we could have at least been happy.'

Her mother smiled a soft knowing smile. 'You love him.'

She nodded, accepting the truth. There was nothing she could do about it. She loved Kazim.

Her mother let her hands go and walked across to the window, looking out over the courtyard garden. A trickle of dread slipped down Amber's spine. 'Mother?'

She watched at her mother returned to her seat, the mask of propriety she always wore back in place after the tender moments of concern for her only daughter.

'I have come for one other reason. Prince Kazim, your husband, sent your father money.' Amber looked at her mother, an unsettling feeling pressing down on her. 'Money that he believes you had requested. He sent it for you, so that you could live your life in comfort.'

Amber tried to take in what she was being told, remembering Kazim's pointed comments about her lack of money, but still it didn't make sense. She met her mother's gaze, tilting her chin in defiant challenge, sensing trouble. She wasn't going to be meek and malleable any more—for anyone.

'Your father has been using it for other causes. He's been funding attacks on Barazbin's people,' her mother finished quickly, her voice almost a whisper as she looked down at her hands, grasped tightly in her lap.

'Why?' Amber asked, moving towards the chair her mother sat in. She wanted to kneel down and look up at her as she'd always done. She couldn't take in this unexpected piece of news.

'He is avenging your honour, Amber.' Her mother spoke softly, her expression intent and serious. 'He believes he is exacting punishment for the way Kazim discarded you.'

'What?' Amber couldn't believe it. All along she'd thought her father had disowned her, but he'd been planning revenge. 'No, he can't be.'

'Please don't say anything!' Her mother looked up beseechingly and Amber saw real panic in her eyes. 'It is misguided loyalty to you, I'm sure, but don't tell your husband. We will all be ruined. Your marriage will be over.'

'Why are you telling me, if I can't tell Kazim?' Amber loved her mother, but she also loved her husband. Her loyalties were being pulled and tested between a family who'd as good as disowned her and a man who didn't love her.

'Because you love him and because I want you to be happy.' Her mother's eyes looked sad despite the forced upbeat tone of her voice.

'How can I not tell him? Keeping one secret has all but destroyed my marriage.' Panic rose up as she met her mother's gaze. She was asking the impossible. She couldn't be loyal to both her husband and her parents.

'I must go,' her mother said and got up, anxiously looking around her. 'Promise me you won't tell him.'

How could her mother ask that of her? 'I don't know,' she whispered honestly. 'I don't know if I can promise you anything.'

'Then, whatever happens, remember I'm here for you.' Her mother touched her arm briefly and Amber had the strangest desire to throw herself into her arms, to be a young child, safe and protected. But she wasn't that child any more.

Amber swallowed down disappointment and watched as her mother turned and walked away. She still sat in disbelief when Kazim returned a short while later. She looked up at him, not knowing what to say. Should she tell him what she'd just learnt? His comments about how she'd been living when they were in London now made so much more sense. All along she'd thought he'd been referring to the cost of Claude's treatment, as if he begrudged the child a chance at life.

'It is good that your mother has come to welcome you back,' he said as he sat in the same seat her mother had just vacated. His long legs stretched out before him, unusually relaxed, drawing her attention.

Amber bit back the bitter taste of tears, looking down at her hands clasped much tighter than she'd realised in her lap, just as her mother's had been. What would he say if she told him why her mother had come?

She didn't know what to think, who to be loyal to. Deep down she knew her first loyalty should be to Kazim now, but how could she ignore the plea in her mother's face?

'It is,' she said and looked up into his handsome face, her breath catching when she saw the warm smile on his lips. Inside her, a liquid heat rushed around, making her feel giddy as he continued to watch her, his eyes sparking with unmistakable desire. She nearly gave in, but sense prevailed.

'I have more good news,' he said as he sat forward, bringing them close enough for her to catch the heady masculine scent of the desert, stronger now.

What else was he going to throw at her? 'Is it news from Annie?' Hope leapt in her chest. She was desperate to hear from her friend.

He frowned and the excitement she'd momentarily felt seeped away. 'You will hear soon. Hasim is looking after them, do not fear. The news I have is more important,' he said quickly, as if trying to distract her. 'Tonight there will be a feast here in the palace, in honour of your return.'

'A feast?' This was the last thing she'd expected. She'd been hoping to remain as low profile as possible, not wanting to give false hope to anyone that she would stay around. Least of all to herself.

'Word has gone out swiftly and people are celebrating your return. It is a good sign.' He reached out and took her hand in his, the heat of his skin scorching hers, making her breath catch. 'You are very much wanted in Barazbin and not just by the people.'

'I am?' Why was he saying such things?

He leant forward and took her hand in his, lifting it to his lips, pressing them lightly against the back of her hand, making her heart flutter wildly. 'You are mine now,' he said in a husky whisper, his eyes sparking with a challenge that mixed with desire, creating a lethal cocktail. 'Truly mine.'

This wasn't about anything more than possession. He'd claimed her as his wife with such dedicated charm he'd been assured success. There would be no question of an annulment now and divorce wasn't on his agenda. He'd made that perfectly clear. She was effectively trapped here with him. A man she loved and found ever harder to resist who only wanted her in the line of duty.

'I will only stay until Annie and Claude return from America,' she interjected fiercely, pulling her hand back, but his fingers held hers tightly, preventing it.

He stood up, his regal command instantly back in place. 'That was never part of our deal, Amber. You agreed to return to Barazbin and you will stay.'

'No,' she snapped, and she pulled her hand away.

'No?' he questioned, his desire-laden eyes hardening to glittering black. 'You will stay and tonight you will go to the feast.'

'I can't. It would be wrong to give the people false hope.' She couldn't keep the pleading note from entering her voice.

From the grim line of his lips she knew it was futile to beg and plead. Instead, she glared at him, seeing his expression turn as heavy as storm clouds. He stood, towering over her, reminding her of his power.

'I shall escort you to the feast. Be ready by sunset.'

Kazim turned and marched from the room, away from the woman who'd practically driven him mad with desire. He had thought her allure would fade once he'd tasted the forbidden fruit, but the fact that she was now truly his and his alone only intensified his need for her. She made him want things he could never have, be the person he could never be.

He thought of her insistence on leaving and irritation bubbled inside him. His people had welcomed her and were expecting her to stay. They wanted her to be their princess and one day their queen. He wanted her by his side on the path through life that fate had forged him— the same fate that had led her to him. He also wanted her in his bed at night. Each and every night. This was a new realisation, one he hadn't totally come to terms with.

As afternoon slipped into evening Kazim realised he was going to have to do more to convince Amber that he wanted her to stay. He had amends to make and tonight would give him the perfect opportunity. He would show off his wife to all present, including his father. He wanted to make sure that nobody would ever question the validity of their marriage. But, most of all, he would do it his way; he wouldn't allow himself to be influenced any more by the way his father had treated his mother. The emotional bully who had eventually broken his mother's spirit, forcing her to retreat from everyone until her death, was not something he wanted to be. He didn't want to live beneath that shadow any longer.

Kazim pushed open the doors to their suite a short time later and his breath was taken away by the sight that greeted him. In full traditional dress of stunning gold, Amber shimmered like an oasis in the parched desert. As his silence lengthened she raised her chin in the defiant little gesture he had come to admire. She was out of this world.

'This time,' he said as his heart hammered a little too fast and desire raced in his blood, making his head pound as if Arabian stallions were galloping right over him, 'far more beautiful than exquisite.'

He moved towards her, drawn by an unknown force, watching her delicate face as a flush swept over her exotically high cheekbones. Her brown eyes, enhanced by make-up, watched him boldly and he clenched his fists against the desire to drag her to bed right now and forget the formalities of the banquet. How was he going to be able to spend the entire evening at her side, when all he wanted was her naked and beneath his body in his bed as he claimed her again and again?

'Not without the help of an army of maids.' She smiled, her face suddenly lighting up, her eyes sparkling like the ocean on a sunny day. He had never seen her smile like that, but he liked it and vowed to make it happen more often.

'You are a princess and such treatment goes with the job.' He stood to one side, his hand held out towards the doors. 'If you are ready, Princess Amber of Barazbin, we have to attend a banquet in your honour.'

Shyness rushed over Amber as she walked towards him, as his eyes seemed to devour every part of her body, which sizzled from just his gaze. It was madness, but she wanted him with such a force it almost knocked her breath from her body.

Focus, she told herself as, a few minutes later, they entered the banqueting hall, which was adorned with flowers and where a scent of spices filled the air. Voices hummed to a hush as she entered with Kazim, curious eyes cast her way. What were they thinking? Were they really welcoming her with open arms?

Such thoughts raced through her mind as

the festivities erupted around her; dancers and beautiful music filled the magnificent room that formed the centre of the palace. Captivated, she stopped and looked around her, feeling Kazim stop at her side, his arm pulling her just that little bit closer.

'This is for you, Princess Amber.' His voice, velvety soft as he spoke close to her ear, sent shivers down her spine. 'They are welcoming you home.'

Her heart thumped in her chest and she turned to look into his handsome face, now so tantalisingly close. 'I am honoured.'

'Before we enjoy the evening, my father would like to welcome you back.' Was it just her imagination or had his voice hardened, just from the mention of his father? Before she had time to say anything he guided her through the throng of people, all smiling her way and eager to catch her attention. She smiled back with graceful dignity and followed, but inside quaked at the thought of seeing her father-in-law again. Kazim's revelations about his childhood only reinforced her first impression of the man: hard, mean and relentless.

'I see my son has succeeded.' Sheikh Amir Al Amed fixed her with a piercing glare and Amber met it head-on, taking in the implication of his words.

'Did you doubt him?' She couldn't help herself. She wasn't going to stand meekly before him and allow him to intimidate her. Kazim's arm loosened on hers. She'd spoken out of turn.

Kazim's father looked first at his son with narrowed eyes then back to her and she felt the full force of his scrutiny.

'I'm pleased to see you are feeling stronger today, Father,' Kazim interjected into the conversation. 'It does us both a great honour that you are present this evening.'

Kazim's gallant words salved his father's prickly demeanour, but she knew he was doing what came naturally. He was stepping in, protecting her. Just as he'd done for his mother and because of that he'd got hurt. The scar on his chest bore testament to that. Her heart softened and instinctively she moved closer to Kazim.

Sheikh Amir nodded in satisfaction, keeping his eyes firmly on Amber. 'I made a wise choice with your marriage.'

'You did,' Amber boldly answered and felt Kazim turn to look at her, but she kept her eyes locked with his father.

She blinked in shock when Sheikh Amir laughed a deep, throaty laugh and for a brief moment she saw the handsome man he must have once been. 'A wise choice indeed. Now go. Do your duty.'

Dismissed, she allowed Kazim to guide her across the room full of people, her knees suddenly weak from the encounter with his father.

'You've won him over,' Kazim whispered in her ear as the music became louder and the dancing more lively. He gestured to her to sit as they took their places for the festivities. 'I should have known you would. You won me over just as easily.'

Amber was saved from replying by a dancing display before them. Women in bright colours, adorned with gold jewellery, swayed and danced as the music soared to the domed roof of the palace. It was spectacular and took on a dreamlike quality. To think, just a few days ago she was waitressing in Paris, saving for the art course she had enrolled in...

Soon the most delicious food she'd ever tasted began to be served and she made polite conversation with those around her. Every move she made, she could feel Kazim's eyes on her, hot and passionate, openly devouring her. Even when he was apparently deep in conversation with others she felt his gaze slide to her, slip down her body as if he was removing every piece of silk from her.

The torment continued for several hours and, just when she thought she couldn't take it any more, Kazim came and stood next to her, took her hand and led her away from the festivities, just as he had done on their wedding night.

Panic sluiced over her as she wondered what would happen when they were alone. Would he retreat to his sumptuous room within their suite? Cold fear trickled down her spine, as if she were beneath an icy shower. She hadn't mentioned the money, hadn't told him what her mother had come to tell her about how her father was using Kazim's money.

All those thoughts left her mind as he turned to look at her, the black depths of his eyes swirling with unashamed passion.

'This is what should have happened on our wedding night,' he said as he closed the doors of their suite and gathered her up into his arms, marching into his room and placing her on the bed.

'I thought we'd already had our wedding night, in England,' she teased, swept away with the moment. She totally forgot her earlier decision of adopting cool aloofness as he pulled off his headdress, revealing tousled dark hair that her fingers itched to slide into.

'I am making amends for the past and tonight, here in my palace, in Barazbin we shall have our wedding night.'

He moved towards the bed and a rush of

heated desire swept over her, but his next words doused the flame of passion almost instantly.

'Tomorrow I am going into the desert.'

He was leaving her? She couldn't face being alone in the palace now. Despite the fact that until tonight he'd only tolerated her presence out of duty, she wanted to be with him. 'I'd like to come.'

'It is not a place for a princess.' He looked at her, shock evident on his face.

His words didn't deter her, not once the idea had taken shape in her mind, but as he pulled off his robes, revealing his glorious body she had to focus on what he'd said.

She should tell him about the money her father had taken from him on false pretences, but as he strode, almost naked, towards the bed, all thoughts of that left her mind.

'I need to be seen with you—is that not what you said in England?' She pushed her argument forward, trying not to give into the fire which raged inside her body as he lay on the bed next to her, propping himself up with one hand and sliding the other over her silk-covered body. 'Take me with you.'

'The desert is not a place for a princess and, besides, I live like a nomad whilst out there.' His hand trailed seductively over her breasts and her nipples hardened in immediate response. He smiled. A knowing and sexy smile.

'Would it not help your cause if I came with you?' She purred the question at him as her body moved in answer to his caress. 'I could keep you warm at night.'

Instantly his mouth claimed hers in a hard and passionate kiss, which left her reeling from its intensity. His hands pulled at the sumptuous gold silk impatiently and she pressed herself against his nakedness, feeling more powerful, more attractive than she ever had before.

This was the man she loved with all her heart and she wanted to be with him wherever he went, despite all she'd said and promised herself.

'Temptress,' he growled as finally the silk gave way and his hands found her skin. His touch burnt as his fingers caressed her breast.

'Please, Kazim, I want to go with you.' He kissed her again and she wound her arms about his neck, surrendering to the moment. When the kiss ended she whispered seductively, 'Take me with you.'

'What man could refuse such an offer?'

CHAPTER EIGHT

THE HEAT OF the desert was far more intense than Amber remembered. Or was it the man who was now steering the four-wheel drive across the blistering expanse of sand which stretched for miles ahead of them that was causing the intensity? Memories of yet another night in Kazim's arms made her pulse race and she stole a glance at his profile; lines of concentration were furrowing his brow.

All her planned indifference to him was forgotten, lost in the passion he'd brought to life within her with just one glance, one touch. She loved him and as she had to be here in Barazbin at the moment she was going to make the most of it. Certain he didn't love her, she needed to make each and every one of those moments last her a lifetime.

'I'd forgotten how beautiful the desert is,' she said, focusing her attention on the massive sand dunes rising up on either side of them, dominating the intense blue of the skyline. She had the impression that she and Kazim were small and insignificant, pawns in a much bigger game being played out against the majestic landscape.

'It can also be a dangerous place. Just one storm and everything you see will change. The desert is like life—changeable. One storm and the whole course of life alters.' She looked at him, startled.

Was he was referring to his father? This was the closest he'd come to telling her about what had happened. Her eyes were drawn to the way his fingers gripped hard onto the steering wheel, as if the vehicle could give him strength.

Her heart lurched in her chest and she started to reach out to him, wanting to touch him, reassure him, but the look he shot her when he saw her movement killed that thought instantly. He was back behind his line of defence. Once again unreachable.

'What happened?' she asked, hating the hesitation in her voice because whatever it was affected her and she had a right to know. 'The night you got that scar?'

'It is no concern of yours.' His eyes met hers briefly as the vehicle swayed endlessly across the barren gold landscape. The intensity of the angry sparks in the deep blackness of his eyes almost made her hold her tongue. But why should she?

'It is, Kazim. It has implications for me—for us.'

He looked ahead again and she did the same, as if keeping her eyes from his handsome profile would help.

'As I said at the polo match, I stood between my mother and father.'

His voice was hard and level. She could feel the control he was exerting, feel it in the tension that had suddenly filled the vehicle, and all she wanted to do was get out of it, but ahead of her was nothing but sand dunes, sculpted by the hand of Mother Nature.

Amber sighed in frustration, not just at the lengthy and incredibly hot journey but at his reluctance to talk to her. Obviously the hours in each other's arms these last few nights meant nothing. He didn't want her to get close, not emotionally. He had only been staking his claim on her, preventing her from returning to the life she'd made since leaving the desert.

Should she now tell him about the money her father had deceived him over? The money that Kazim had thought he was giving to her? What would he say when he found out her father was attacking Barazbin as a way of avenging the dishonour Kazim had brought upon her by discarding her after their wedding? Judging by the frown on her mother's face yesterday morning, it was not what Kazim would have expected or wanted.

'Kazim, I think we should talk,' she said and looked again at his profile; it was stern and unapproachable. Her courage floundered instantly but she had to tell him.

Kazim wanted to close his eyes against the pain of that day, but he knew he had to explain. She was right—it had implications for both of them. She did have a right to know.

'Very well,' he said, refusing to look at her, keeping his eyes on the way ahead as if he was driving a precarious cliff road instead of the vast sands before them. 'It was my fault.'

'What?' That one word almost squeaked from her lips, heightening his pain and guilt. She sounded shocked.

'It was my fault. I lost my temper. I challenged my father and whilst youth was on my side, experience wasn't.'

He hadn't said so many words at once about that day, not even to his mother, and especially not to his father. Since the day he'd stood up to his father, Kazim and his mother had barely spoken. He'd disappointed her.

Instead of protecting his mother, as he'd done

since he was a boy, he'd let her down. He'd become as bad as the man she'd married. Now, as he drove across the expanse of the desert with Amber at his side it was as if someone had unlocked a door, letting all the pain and guilt spill out from him.

'I'm sure that's not true,' she said softly and touched his arm and his body stiffened. He didn't deserve her sympathy.

He wanted to stop, to turn and give her his full attention. He wanted to tell her everything, but at the same time he didn't want to see the pity that must be swimming in her eyes turn to shame and repulsion. Suddenly, for the first time ever, it mattered what she thought of him.

Instead, he fixed his eyes back on the sand, knowing that very soon they would reach the camp and the luxurious tent he'd instructed to be built in readiness for them. Then he would have to face whatever was in her eyes. Face it and deal with it.

'After you left I wanted to leave too,' he began as the tension built around them to almost explosive levels. He'd envied her the ability to turn and walk away. 'I had no wish to be a prince in a palace, little more than an animal in a cage. I wanted freedom.'

She sat silently next to him and he sensed her shock, sensed the stiffening of her body as

she pulled her hand back. In that moment he realised she'd been the same, a bird in a beautiful prison, manipulated by her parents and then
harshly rejected by him.

He'd started the sorry tale now, so he had to
finish. 'My father and I quarrelled and, before
he left, he accused me of neglecting my people.
He told me the nomad tribes needed help. But
I didn't stay, didn't listen to a word. I had my
own duty, an oil company employing hundreds.
I chose that, never imagining the palace without
my father's heavy hand ruling it.'

'Then your father became ill.' Her voice was
barely a whisper and hardly audible above the
hum of the engine.

'Yes, and my life changed again. Like the
dunes after a sandstorm, no trace of what was
there before was left.' He kept his eyes fixed on
the way ahead.

Amber couldn't comprehend what Kazim was
telling her. 'It still wasn't your fault.'

'True, but if I had not argued, refused to go
back to the palace, he would never have had the
heart attack.'

The four-wheel drive climbed up a large sand
dune, taking all his concentration. She waited—
for what, she didn't know. Then, as they reached
the top of the sand dune, she saw a camp below

them, sheltered on all sides by other high dunes. Many tents spread out before her, people busily going about their daily tasks.

Kazim stopped the vehicle and turned to look at her. 'The thing that hurts the most, after this episode—' he touched his chest, where the scar lay concealed beneath his robes '—my last words to my mother were ones of anger. She refused to see me again and died alone. I destroyed her and never made my peace with her. I cannot forgive myself for that.'

'Don't blame yourself, Kazim. I don't.'

'You should do. Just as you should because I cannot offer you the freedom you crave. The freedom you deserve.'

'I have always known that I would marry a man of my father's choosing. I was never free, Kazim. Neither were you. As you said, it is our duty.'

A duty I do now, first and foremost because of what you can offer to Annie's little boy.

That was her only motivation. It had been what had driven her to accept his hard bargain and now it was what kept her focused. She was here, doing this, for Annie and Claude.

She wanted to ask about them, wanted to know where they were, what they were doing, but now was not the time. Just as it wasn't the time to tell him about the money her father had kept from her. But she would have to tell him.

'Now you know what has happened I do not want to talk of it again.' His words were firm and insistent and her heart wrenched at the pain evident within them. If silence on the subject was what he wanted, that was what she would give him.

'Is this where we will camp?' She injected as much lightness into her voice as she could. The tension swirling around them was almost impossible to bear.

He looked across at her, his eyes piercing into hers, and for a moment she thought she saw shards of raw pain. Then, as if night had fallen, the shutters came down and he was once more fully in command of his emotions, having locked them neatly away.

'This is to be our home for the next week,' he said and started driving towards the camp.

A tremor of panic tore down Amber's spine. Was she really to be here with Kazim for a week? What had she let herself in for during her moment of weakness? A moment when she'd thought she had to be with him, as if the love she had for him could grow inside his heart too, until he couldn't help but tell her he loved her.

Would she ever hear those words from his lips? She frowned at an unwanted childhood memory. She'd never heard those words from anyone other than her grandmother. Nobody else had ever told her they loved her. She'd thought her mother had hinted at it the last time they'd spoken. But she never displayed affection. Why should that change now?

This was madness.

'We have our own tent at the outer edge of the camp.' He pointed towards a larger, much grander tent than the small and unassuming ones dotted around them as they drove into the camp.

As they neared the tent she could see theirs was far from small, far from plain. In fact it appeared to be a palace of fabric. 'I thought you said you didn't do luxury in the desert.' She was too shocked to keep the words to herself and was rewarded with a light and very sexy laugh as he stopped the vehicle at the side of the tent.

'I don't, but you do.'

She got out of the vehicle, glad to stretch her legs after the tense journey, and walked a little closer, unable to believe such luxury here in the middle of the desert. It was like something from a tale from long ago. A tale of seduction.

'I didn't have to,' she said as she walked towards their tent, stopping a little way off, totally amazed.

Amber had never seen anything like it. The

front of the tent was pulled back and she could
see inside. Deep purple curtains hung within
it and rich gold cushions were scattered on the
carpet. Lanterns glowed, lighting the dim interior, and the heady scent of incense teased her
senses as it drifted on the breeze. She turned to
Kazim earnestly. 'I could have stayed in something more modest.'

He stood behind her, his hands resting on her
shoulders, heat rushing from him and igniting
the desire they'd shared last night. 'I want you
to stay here with me. I want you to be truly my
desert princess.'

His deep voice was slow and incredibly sexy
and she could feel his breath on her ear before
he bent and kissed her neck. She closed her eyes
against the rising flow of desire. Was this his
way of distracting her from what they'd just
spoken of? Would he do this every time she got
just that bit too close to the real man?

Part of her hoped that he would, but another
part of her knew it wouldn't last, that he would
soon tire of her and seek comfort and satisfaction elsewhere, return to his playboy prince role
and become the oil sheikh that women dreamt
of being with and men wanted to emulate.

'I have a meeting with the elders of the camp,'
he said as he drew her into the privacy of the

tent and took her in his arms. 'But when I return we will be together all night.'

The promise, given in such a sexy deep voice, made her heart hammer against her chest. Hot liquid warmth erupted from deep within her, igniting desire again. With just one caress, a kiss and a few soft words he'd melted her, crumbling any resistance she had—because she loved him. Even more so now she'd glimpsed the real man, seen that he felt, that he cared and that he loved. All she could hope for now was that he would one day love her.

But would he? Would he ever truly be hers and love her as she'd loved him since the day she'd been told by her father that he would be her husband, her prince? If he couldn't, she knew she'd have to leave.

'I will be here,' she said seductively and reached up to press her lips against his.

'What man could refuse such an offer,' he said between kisses that stirred their passion to new heights. 'It is my hope that our union will soon be blessed with an heir.'

Have his baby? The thought settled over her, creating images of a child with dark hair, so like Kazim. The idea of having his child, his heir, when he didn't love her, cast the preceding moments into shadow.

'You want children? So soon?' She pulled back and looked up at him, her voice a husky whisper.

His eyes met hers; the sparks of desire swirling in them made her heart race and she fought against it. This was important and not at all what she had bargained on. Having a child now would tie them irrevocably together. Inside, she breathed a sigh of relief, thankful she'd been taking precautions of her own. She wasn't at all sure she was ready to be tied to this man for the rest of her life, not when he didn't love her.

'Of course.' His brow rose then his eyes narrowed slightly. 'I am heir to the throne of Barazbin. The only heir. I have to produce my own heir!' He looked at her, making her breath catch as his eyes darkened, the molten gold flecks more pronounced than ever. 'It is our duty, Amber. The reason we married.'

'I just hadn't expected it to be so soon.' Her pulse rate increased as he stroked the back of his fingers gently down her cheek, his thumb lingering teasingly on her lips.

'We have been married almost one year, Amber.'

'I know; it's just that I…'

'That you what, Amber? Wanted to run back to your life in Paris as soon as you thought you'd done your duty? As soon as my side of the deal was completed and Claude had had all the operations he needed?'

She took a deep breath. That was exactly what she'd thought. She blinked, realising that for the first time Kazim hadn't referred to Claude as 'the child'.

'Is there any news about Claude?' She grasped at the offered change of subject, anything rather than discuss what existed between them, something that would mean she'd never be free.

It wasn't that she didn't want children, or even Kazim's children. It was simply that she wanted to be loved and needed for herself, not out of a sense of duty or because she would bear the kingdom of Barazbin its future ruler. But, most importantly, she wanted to love and be loved in return—without any constraints.

Kazim smiled down at her as if he knew he'd caught her attention. 'Your friend and her son are in America right now. He is scheduled for his first operation in two days. As soon as we return to the palace you can contact them.'

Relief rushed through her. In part because she'd successfully derailed the discussion on children, and also because things were finally happening for Claude. She was well aware the road to final recovery would be long, but at least Kazim had kept his word and had not only funded the operations but also arranged them.

The only problem now was that she was honour-bound to keep her side of the bargain. But Kazim's talk of an heir was too much. Once again she felt as if everything was closing in on her, forcing her down a route she wasn't happy to take.

'I wish you'd told me it was happening.' She tried to keep her focus off her problems. 'I've been worried for Annie, worried she'll think I have run out on her. I didn't explain anything.'

He laughed softly, a deep genuine laugh that stirred the desire his closeness had evoked. 'I'm told she is happy for you and is looking forward to seeing you again. Hasim is looking after her, taking his role very seriously—as I knew he would.'

Amber blushed. 'Thank you, Kazim.'

Kazim smiled down at Amber and what was now becoming a familiar tightening across his chest happened once more. The strange new emotions were all consuming, but even so he didn't want to analyse them now. If he did, something would go wrong, just as it always did when he got emotionally close to people.

He'd lost too much already. First a father who had almost dismissed him out of hand as a young boy, then his mother, because he'd been as brutal as his father. The guilt of that was now so raw after the drive into the desert this morning. He still didn't understand why he'd opened up, why he'd said so much to Amber.

He looked at her, a gentle colour heightening her cheeks, those mysterious eyes of hers almost veiled by her long lashes as she cast her eyes down.

'We don't need to talk about heirs right now,' he said and lifted her chin so that he could see clearly into her eyes, try and fathom the emotions that ran so deep within them yet always managed to perplex him, muddling his own feelings.

'No,' she whispered so softly he almost didn't catch it. 'You need to go to your meeting.'

To hell with the meeting, he wanted to say, but it was his duty—a duty he took very seriously—and now he was duty-bound to finish what his father had started.

He clenched his jaw against the guilt that rushed through him, sweeping every other emotion to one side, including the warm, tender feelings for Amber. At the same time he sensed her withdrawal, saw the shutters come down over her eyes, blocking him out.

Should he have just sought her out in Paris and insisted on a divorce—something she'd been more than willing to do? Reclaiming his wife would not only resolve the issue of his ability to be the heir and continue the family line, but he'd always hoped, yet never admitted, that in doing so he would also regain just a little bit of his father's respect. Although why he sought respect from a man who'd bullied everyone he should have loved was still very much a mystery.

'Later we will have much to discuss, Amber,' he said as he let go of her, his body instantly missing the warmth of hers. 'We have the future of Barazbin in our hands. Whatever we do will affect so many people. We have to get it right.'

'I know,' she said, her chin lifting defiantly, her eyes calmly fixing on his, her tone resigned. 'It is our duty.'

CHAPTER NINE

DUTY.

The word tasted sour in her mouth and, as dusk had given way to darkness, Amber began to doubt what she was doing. Had she been right to expect she could turn her back on Barazbin and walk away from Kazim? Everything had suddenly become much more complicated than it had seemed as they'd stood talking about it in the small flat in Paris.

If she wasn't marooned in the desert she would probably want to get the first plane home. But where was home? Annie and Claude were in America, and her father still showed no interest in reconciliation, despite her mother's impromptu visit and unexplained message.

Outside the tent she heard voices and hurried activity as the wind picked up, but was too distracted with her thoughts to give it much more than a fragment of her attention. Instead, she made her way into one of the large bedrooms that was hung with deep purple and gold cloth. It was most definitely regal and every comfort had been catered for. The bed, although almost at floor level, was large and sumptuous, adorned with so many cushions of gold and purple she wondered if she should just curl up among them. It was late and tiredness made the prospect of doing exactly that so very enticing, but the heat in Kazim's eyes when they had arrived stopped her. He'd said he'd wanted her to stay here with him. Each word had been full of the promise of possession and, right now, she wanted that. Wanted to be with him, share the midnight hours with the man she loved and pretend he loved her back.

At that moment, as if conjured up by a dream, Kazim pulled back the curtains that served as a door and walked in, his presence totally overwhelming the splendour of the tent. The incense that had earlier smelt so uplifting had become masked by his intoxicating scent, desert mixed with musky aftershave. Her heart started the pounding it always did when he was near but, remembering their parting discussion, she stood tall, the strength of her gaze locking with his.

Was he here in her quarters of this lavish tent out of a sense of duty, as his parting words to her had suggested? Or did he want to continue what he'd started at the polo weekend? Questions whirred in her mind. Had that night been his dutiful seduction routine? His quest for an heir?

'Should we continue discussing our duty towards your country?' Her words, sharper than any blade, were delivered with fierce accuracy as those last thoughts sank in.

He didn't flinch, his steady gaze, as hard as obsidian, never left her face. He stepped into the sanctuary of her quarters, allowing the curtain to fall back into place behind him, cocooning them in a world as unreal as anything she'd ever known.

'When were you going to tell me, Amber?' His question was delivered with slow precision and she blinked against the icy tone of each word, unable to decipher what he meant.

'Tell you what, exactly?' Not sure how to answer, she tried for nonchalance but, with her heart hammering wildly just from seeing him standing, raw and potent, before her, she knew she hadn't pulled it off. If anything, she'd sounded guilty. But guilty of what?

'That you and your father have been funding the rebel attacks on my people.' His face darkened as if storm clouds had rolled in across the desert and at any moment she expected a crack of thunder and a flash of lightning before a deluge of rain. But he remained as firm and resolute as before, condemnation etched deep into his handsome face.

Amber stood motionless and took in his words, the harsh accusation in his eyes watching her every move. Even when she blinked she was sure he was aware of it. It didn't make sense. She had hardly had enough money to live this past year, having not had any help from anyone, not even her parents. Just how had he come up with the idea that she and her father were paying rebels to attack his people?

'Who told you that?' Like a lioness on the prowl she pounced to deny the charge, throwing her own question back at him. How dare he come marching into her quarters insinuating she was behind such a thing?

'It doesn't matter who told me—what matters is your answer. So I will ask again. When were you going to tell me that you have been using the money I sent to your father, for you to live in a manner befitting your role as my princess, to support the rebels?' He moved closer to her, unnerving her with every glance, every stride. It wasn't his obvious anger but much more the man himself—a man she wanted and loved, but a man who only wanted her out of duty.

'Whatever it is my father has done, I have had no part in,' she said and tossed her head to flick her hair from her face, the movement drawing his eyes, his scrutiny.

She thought of her mother's visit, the bizarre claim that it would ruin them if Kazim found out. She'd looked anxious and for the first time Amber wondered if her mother was more afraid of the man she'd married than she was of the man she'd married her daughter to. She closed her eyes briefly, knowing she should have told Kazim as soon as her mother had left. She should have pushed aside any ill placed loyalty for her father. So why hadn't she?

The look of terror on her mother's face, the tremor in her voice, the like of which she'd never seen her mother display before, had held her back.

'Is it not true you knew he'd used my money and you didn't even tell me? Instead, you acted as if you were a complete spendthrift when we were in London.' He stopped talking and looked at her, as if willing her to say something else, to deny his words. But they were in part true. She had let him think she was looking for more money, more gifts.

She'd let him think the worst of her out of self-preservation. What she hadn't told him was that she'd never seen any of the money he'd sent to her and that her father had kept it all. She hadn't even known about the money until those first comments in Paris. His questions hadn't been direct, but still she'd hidden behind the lie. She'd been protecting her heart then and now she was saying nothing out of loyalty to her mother.

Kazim swore harshly and strode to the far side of the tent before turning quickly. 'Damn it, Amber, I trusted you! I believed every word you said when all along you were only after as much as you could get.'

She watched in stunned silence as he ploughed his fingers through his thick dark hair and wondered if there was anything she could say to sort this. But whatever she said would expose her true feelings for him, so wasn't it for the best, just as she'd thought in Paris, for him to think the worst of her—that she was a money-hungry woman? At least then they could go their separate ways.

Her heart broke at the thought, but she knew it would be harder and a much bigger heartbreak if she stayed with him any longer. She shouldn't have agreed to return to Barazbin. 'You should never have come to find me, Kazim.'

'I was a fool for thinking you could be part of my life, part of the future of Barazbin. A damn fool.' His angry words resounded around the rich heavy fabric and her legs weakened until she thought she was going to collapse into a heap in the middle of the cushions.

'I was the fool for ever agreeing to the marriage in the first place.' Anger fizzed into her veins, giving life to new strength. 'I don't want to be a burdensome duty for anyone. I just want to be happy.'

'Happy.' That one word, spoken with his heavy accent, seemed to shake the whole tent and she glanced around her as every piece of the fabric wall moved and swayed. 'To be happy is not on our wish list, Amber. We have a duty to our countries, our families.'

'Just like you had a duty to seduce me with tender caresses and sweet words? Was it your duty to secure the future of Barazbin by producing an heir—without informing me?' She glared at him, hands on hips, the rising tide of anger peaking. 'Well, I am sorry to tell you, but there will not be an heir as on those nights we spent together I was using contraception.'

He rounded on her so fast she stepped back into the scattered pillows, almost stumbling on them. 'Yet more deception.' His angry words were slow and purposeful. 'Is there no end to the lengths you will go to?'

'If you had told me before I agreed to return with you that producing an heir was necessary I would have told you I couldn't do that.' She watched as his face hardened, his lips pressing into a thin line. 'I would have said no, no matter what tantalising blackmail you used.'

'Your accusation of blackmail is becoming tiresome.' He stepped ever closer to her, towering over her, but she refused to be intimidated and stood her ground, looking up into his face and deep into the depths of his eyes, now so glacial. 'But I cannot tolerate your deception.'

'My deception!' Amber gasped out the words and, as if in echo to her shock, the fabric walls billowed again with the fury of a force far greater than their anger. Shouts could be heard, orders being barked out and people running. She watched as he looked around, saw his eyes narrow in suspicion and then his jaw clench. She wanted to reach out to him, to ask him for reassurance but, from the worried look on his face, she doubted he could give her any.

She knew the wind had picked up. She might have spent most of her adult life in Europe, but she knew the desert winds were capable of coming out of nowhere. Kazim's earlier talk of the ever changing desert came back to her, and the panicked shouts of men outside worried her. Something was very wrong.

Kazim looked around him, his attention diverted by the way the tent billowed in, making the gold fabric shimmer in the light from the lantern. The wind had picked up but something far worse was happening out there. His gaze rested again on Amber, the anger he'd experienced at her deception receding like the tide. He'd brought her to the desert and could well have put her in danger. Once again, someone he was close to was going to be hurt. He adamantly refused to look deeper into that thought.

'Stay here.' He took hold of her arms and forced her to look at him. 'Do you hear me? Stay here.'

'What is it?' she asked, her words laced with panic. He knew he'd scared her more than necessary.

'I will be back in a few minutes but, whatever you do, stay here.' He injected as much urgency into his voice as possible and the heat of her arms beneath his hands grounded him somehow.

Before he had time to reconsider he left her, tossing aside the curtain to her quarters roughly, and made his way to the main entrance of the tent, now secured for the night. Quickly he opened it and one look outside told him all he needed to know. Nature was taunting them with the threat of a sandstorm, but the frenzied activities of the nomads suggested only one thing.

They were under attack.

'Kazim?'

He swore and turned to face Amber as she now stood in the main living quarters. 'Can you ever do as you are told?' With harsh movements he secured the tent entrance again and hoped the rebels wouldn't attack in full force. He was torn. Stay with Amber or go to the nomads?

'What's happening?' Her voice quivered with fear but he was still angry that she hadn't heeded his warning and stayed where she was. In her quarters at the back of the tent was the best place for both of them to be.

'A desert storm is threatening.'

'But it could get worse, right?' She looked at him, her face imploring him to tell the truth. *Truth! Would she know what that was?*

'It already has.'

'What do you mean?' Panic entered her voice once again, and guilt tugged at him.

'The rebels are out there too. Attack is imminent.'

Her eyes widened in shock, but she didn't say anything.

Quickly, he took her arm and propelled her towards her quarters. 'We will go back to where I told you to stay and sit it out. That is the safest and best option.' His hand locked around hers, almost dragging her back into her quarters as the fabric walls billowed and the wind wailed mournfully around them.

He pulled her down onto the bed, tossing aside some of the cushions in exasperation. 'We just wait and hope. The threatening storm may be our saviour.'

'That's it?' she snapped and turned to face him, suddenly so very close that his chest tightened and for a moment he couldn't say anything. 'That's your master plan?'

Amber clung to his arm and he closed his eyes against the raging emotions inside him. She was seeking his protection; even if she didn't utter a word, her actions told him that. His mind raced back in time, to the moment he'd failed to protect his mother. He could hear her scream and feel the fiery pain in his chest as he was pushed against the sharp corner of a marble statue pedestal.

'Kazim, someone's trying to get in.' Amber's panicked words hurtled him back to the present and he leapt to his feet, preparing to defend.

Relief surged through him as the son of the nomad elder rushed in, his words as hurried as his entrance.

'What is it?' Amber asked as the nomad quickly left. 'Do you need to go?'

He shook his head, trying to regain his usual control, thankful that the wind had played its part to their advantage. 'They have gone. It seems the wind is mistress of the desert tonight.'

She sighed in relief. 'Are you sure they won't come back?'

'Not tonight,' he said as he sat next to her, wanting to hold her. 'All we need to worry about now is the wind and staying safe.'

'Are you trying to seduce me?' she teased and his pulse rate rocketed into overdrive.

'I would not be deceitful enough to use the cover of an impending storm—neither would I need to.' He looked deep into her eyes, trying to fathom the emotions that were buried within them. The truth was: he did want to seduce her. With every cell in his body he wanted her; despite everything, he still craved the release being with her could give him.

The intensity of that lust was something he'd never experienced before. Usually the novelty of a woman wore off once he'd bedded her, but with Amber it was different. Was that because he'd waited so long to claim her, to then discover that she too had waited and that she was truly his?

'I wasn't trying to deceive you, Kazim,' she said softly as her gaze lowered, those long lashes covering her eyes, hiding her soul from his scrutiny. But her apology only raised more questions.

'On our wedding day you tried to be something which I now know you were not. Now I discover you knew of your father's allegiance with the rebels. How can I ever trust you?'

If he could walk away from her at this minute he would. But he couldn't. They were trapped together in this tent and, judging by the sound of the wind outside, they would be for some time yet. Could he turn it to his advantage? Find out the truth about the woman he'd married, once and for all?

Amber sighed. Did he not trust anything she'd said or done? 'From day one of our marriage it was doomed. You didn't want to believe me; you only wanted to believe what you saw—or what you thought you saw.'

'What I saw then and still see now is a woman who was very proficient at weaving a web of lies. The same woman who is unable to deny the facts I've just presented her with. You do not know truth.' His words were slow but firm and she glanced up at his profile, his handsome face drawn into a mask of concentration.

Around them the wind buffeted the tent, seemingly determined to gain entry. Nervously she watched the fabric shifting ominously in the low light from the lanterns. It should be romantic, a time for two lovers to come together and lose themselves from the outside world.

But they were not lovers. What they shared

was an undeniable spark of attraction—one that demanded satisfaction and one she was sure would fade in time until it was nothing more than glowing coals amidst a dying fire.

'I was doing my duty, Kazim. Surely you, of all people, can relate to that?' They had been forced together by the might of the desert and he had to listen to her, had to see why she'd acted as she had. She pressed on before he added anything and distracted her from her mission. 'It was made very clear to me that, to inherit your father's kingdom, it was of the utmost importance that our marriage went ahead.'

'That, at least, is true.' He picked up a gold cushion, absently examining the braiding. Anything other than look at her it seemed. 'I was told much the same. As long as we consummated the marriage it did not matter if we lived together afterwards or not—for a while, at least. That is the only reason I agreed to it.'

'But you weren't even able to consummate the marriage.' Anger burst to life once more inside her, rushing through her veins so insistently she wanted to get up off the bed and run as far away as possible. She fought the urge with everything she had. 'Why was that, Kazim? Did you hate me that much?'

'No!' He rounded on her, furiously throwing the cushion aside. 'I hated that we were forced to marry. I had a life. I'd built up a successful business. I never wanted to inherit.'

He took a deep breath and looked at her and she waited, biting down on her lip anxiously.

'I didn't want responsibility either for the people of Barazbin or for you. I didn't want to desire you or make you truly my wife because you represented all that I resented.'

His harsh words hit hard and she blinked in shock. He really did dislike her and certainly hated the fact that they had been forced to marry. As soon as she could she would leave this country, this man, and go back home to Paris.

'I had no knowledge of what my father was doing,' she pushed on, needing to clear her name, but not wanting to cause any problems for her mother. It wasn't going to be achievable, judging from the look on Kazim's face.

He got up and marched away from her, pacing across the carpet so fast it was as if he would at any moment walk out beyond the tent and into the desert, which she was quickly realising was his mistress.

He turned to her, anger evident in the rigidity of his stance. 'You should have told me.'

Her eyes widened in shock. This was the last thing she'd expected to hear from him and she could barely stammer out the words. 'I couldn't…my mother…' she stammered, feeling as if she was losing her footing.

'Don't try and tell me you didn't know anything about it, that your mother was the one who told you.'

'I didn't.' Her words were a strangled whisper, his nearness and the shock of his accusation clamping tightly on her throat. He didn't believe anything she said and never had.

The blackness of his eyes darkened and the intensity of his gaze became too much and she moved away from him, walking across the carpet as he had just done. Beneath her feet the sand moved, reminding her just how volatile the peace they'd recently shared actually was.

'But you still didn't tell me.' It wasn't a question, but a statement. One filled with regret. 'You had plenty of opportunity to tell me on the drive here.'

'I'm sorry. I didn't realise the importance or significance of what I'd learnt and then you talked of your father. The time didn't feel right.' She wished now she'd insisted she had something important to say, but he'd opened up to her, let her into his world, just for a moment.

'That was a discussion you forced on me.' He gritted his teeth and she knew she was pushing him too far, but suddenly she realised she had to.

Here in this tent, with a sandstorm threatening, she had to force him to face up to his emotions. Maybe then there would be a future together, but if there wasn't she had at least tried. Once and for all she had to admit what was between them. It was up to her, it seemed, to decide just what it was. Suddenly nothing was more important. She had to know what it meant to her, as well as Kazim.

'You lock everyone out, Kazim. Why?'

His breathing deepened but he remained where he was, glaring at her.

'Don't try to analyse my emotions, Amber. That is a game you will not win.'

'This is not a game. This is real.' She moved towards him so that she stood close enough to feel the heat from his body, hear the deep breaths he took.

'Be very careful, Amber.' He growled out the words. 'You might find you're taking on more than you can handle.'

'I can handle this,' she snapped, glad that the simmering tension was finally about to boil over. 'I'm telling you I knew nothing of the money you have been sending to my father. If I did I would never have worked in that club or lived in that flat and it would have been me helping Annie and Claude—me, not you.'

The tirade rushed from her like an avalanche,

gathering speed and power as it went until her heart raced and her head throbbed.

His eyes narrowed in suspicion but before he could say anything she pushed on.

'I admit I came with you to Barazbin because you were going to help Claude, and that I intended to go back to Paris as soon as I could. But I also came because I needed to explore what is between us and because, deep down, I wanted to.'

'You wanted to?' He looked at her in complete disbelief. 'That is as far from the truth as you can possibly get. As soon as I found you in that club you were talking of a divorce.'

'Because I thought that was what you wanted.' The wind seemed to rush at the tent but she didn't take her eyes from his. 'You rejected me, Kazim, and I will never forget how that felt. I tried to be what you wanted, but it wasn't enough. The disgust in your eyes nearly killed me.'

It also nearly killed my love for you.

'I didn't expect my wife to come with a baggage of scandal.' The words snapped from him but she didn't care. The lines of communication had at last been opened. If nothing else, she would find out why he'd turned her away so brutally.

'But I thought...' What had she thought? That

he'd been so enraged to find out she was an in-experienced virgin, he'd turned her away?

'What did you think?' he asked.

'That a man like you would want a more in-teresting wife.'

'No.' He shook his head and took hold of her arms, pulling her closer and forcing her to look up at him. 'I wanted my wife to be mine and mine alone. I know now that you are. Despite the many months we've been apart, you have always been mine.'

This was too much. Her heart began to swoop and soar with hope. Was he opening his heart to her, allowing her in?

'Yes, I have,' she said, scarcely above a whis-per. 'I always have, Kazim. I love you.'

CHAPTER TEN

KAZIM REELED BACK in shock, abruptly letting
her go. Had he heard her right? Amber loved
him? He looked at her face, so beautiful in the
soft light from the lanterns, and that new and
all too familiar tightness gripped his chest. As
he continued to stand, silent from the shock
of those words, anxiety leapt to her eyes. He
wished he could take it away but he couldn't, not
when he was still unable to believe she meant
those words. She hadn't told him one truth yet.

He stepped back a pace, needing distance
from her, from her words. What did she have
to gain by lying? Had she said the one thing he
never wanted to hear to deliberately anger him?
Was this her way of extricating herself from the
marriage? Pushing him to the edge?

'That's not possible.' He stepped back further, unable to deal with her latest little lie or
the emotions it unleashed within him. He had
never wanted to hear those words said to him

again. They meant nothing. His past had taught him they were words used to inflict pain—they were weapons. They were also words he never intended to say to anyone. Never. Love, if it did exist, was not for him.

'Why not?' Her throaty whisper sounded sexy. Too sexy. A rush of lust throbbed inside him, totally contradicting the shock that still surrounded him.

She walked towards him, her soft brown eyes intently watching his face. He wanted to turn and march away from her. But where was there to go? The wind still wailed beyond the tent, even if the rebels had gone. He was trapped.

His gaze lingered on her slender figure and the way the deep red silk wrapped around her body. She'd changed, casting off the jeans and blouse she'd opted to travel in, but he dismissed the idea that it was for him. The red silk shimmered as she took a step towards him and seemed to give her a regal power he'd never noticed before. She stopped, her eyes intently watching his face, waiting for his answer.

What should he say? *I don't want love—from you or anyone.* No, that was getting too close to the truth. Just the thought of saying that aloud made him feel vulnerable.

'Why not?' He repeated her question, knowing he sounded defensive. 'Do you really need to ask?'

'Actually, yes, I do,' she replied, her voice sharper now, which at least had the effect of dampening his ardour.

'You have made it clear that you are here under duress and the only reason is so that your friend's child can have his medical treatment.' He turned things back to her in an attempt to halt her uncomfortable questions. He stood his ground as she moved to stand in front of him, determination coming off her in waves. Was she hell-bent on making him face the past—all of it, in one day?

'So you feel nothing for me?' Boldly, she looked up at him and he had the strange sensation that it wasn't him turning the tables, that he was losing *his* foothold. Somehow he was now the mouse being toyed with by the cat. He didn't like it. Not one bit.

He thought of the tightness that crushed his chest when his mind wandered to her, but that must be panic; it couldn't be love. Love only brought pain. He knew that after the way it had scarred his heart all through his childhood. It couldn't be anything else. After all, as a young man, he had vowed never to love and he had no intention of breaking that vow. He'd seen what one-sided love had done to his mother.

'Love is a fool's indulgence.' He put every bit of anger he had into those words, delivering them with a sharp crack, but Amber stood firm before him, her chin lifted and her shoulders pulled back. Regal defiance emanated from every part of her.

She nodded in agreement. 'You're right.' She looked fiercely into his eyes and he had the sensation she was trying to read his mind, to discover his innermost thoughts. 'A fool's indulgence.'

'Damn it, Amber, don't look at me like that.' He was unable to deal with the power shift that had happened as soon as she'd said those words aloud, giving them life and meaning. He didn't want that. Not now, not ever.

'What are you afraid of, Kazim?' She took another step closer and he inhaled deeply, taking in her soft scent, which reminded him of the palace gardens—the oasis of tranquillity he had come to enjoy during brief interludes from his frantic daily life.

What was he afraid of? That was a question he'd never wanted to answer—until now. The woman he'd married out of duty, the woman who had professed to hate him, was now the woman who was making him face the past head-on.

He didn't want to face it. He couldn't face it.

'It's a useless emotion, Amber. Love serves

no purpose. You and I have married out of duty, and it can't be anything more than that.' Control returned and he looked down into her upturned face, keeping his own devoid of emotion. She must never know the turmoil she'd unleashed with those three words. If she did, it would give her every last bit of power, leaving him completely exposed, and that was not acceptable. He never wanted to experience that harsh vulnerability or to have his inner peace hanging by a thread, one that could be cruelly cut at any time.

'Ah, yes, a duty you took so seriously you couldn't even make me your wife on our wedding night. Was it really the scandalous rumours that disgusted you, or was it the fact that you couldn't do your duty because I wasn't your usual choice of woman and you didn't desire me?'

Her words were granite-hard, laced with a hint of sarcasm like a lethal cocktail. It was as if suddenly she had turned to steel or been sculpted from ice. He didn't really care. At least she wasn't throwing herself at him, professing love as false as the tears that had threatened to wet her cheeks. He couldn't take that sort of emotional display. It was too raw.

'It was nothing more than the fact that I had been led to believe you were an innocent bride.

Exactly what a prince would want.' He spoke firmly, now more in control of the strange sensations that had assailed him when she'd made that ridiculous confession. 'I certainly hadn't been expecting a dancer, especially one so provocative and alluring. It was like I'd stepped back in time and I was a sheikh selecting from his harem. That is something I never wanted to experience.'

It was that image, coupled with the rumours, that had made him turn from her—the image of a bullying sheikh, demanding and unrelenting. A sheikh like his father had been. It was too close to his past.

Her eyes lowered and those lovely long lashes spread over her cheeks and he balled his hands into fists in an effort to stop himself reaching out and touching her, lifting her chin so that he could see her face. If he let his mind continue to wander that path of want and need, he would end up taking her in his arms, kissing her until she begged him to make her his again.

'I'm sorry—about that night, I mean.' She looked shyly up at him and his heart suddenly thumped like a drum. 'In my inexperience, I was doing what I thought right.'

He clenched his fist harder. She was testing him fully. First the soft words, then the fiery determination, then the coyness. What would be next? The tears?

'It's not important any more.' He moved away from her, away from the intoxicating scent of her perfume and the alluring darkness of her eyes, away from the temptation of her soft lips.

'As you wish,' she said, her words quiet but firm.

Amber stood and watched him, his powerful body rigid with discomfort. If her confession of love had made him so uncomfortable, she had no alternative but to insist on returning to Paris and her old life. She would demand a divorce. She wouldn't be any worse off than the moment he'd rejected her on their wedding night.

But you will. The thought lingered in her mind. *You will because you've loved him in every way a woman can, with your heart and your body.*

'Don't play the capitulating woman with me, Amber.' His harsh words wounded more than she was ever prepared to let him know.

She had to concede defeat. Their marriage was doomed. No—it was over. He didn't love her, would never love her if his last words were true, and she just couldn't face living like that. If she went home, back to her life in Paris, she would eventually pick up the pieces, wouldn't she? To love the memory of the man must be better than to live each day with him, knowing he didn't love her.

'I am merely being practical, Kazim. You and I, we can't carry on like this.' It was an effort to keep her voice steady when her heart was pounding so frantically. But if he could be in total command of his emotions, be so cold and harsh, then so could she.

'We have to remain married, Amber. I have a duty to my country to produce an heir. You know that.' His lips set firmly and she noticed the shadow of stubble on his chin. Her mind, totally unable to process what he'd just said, instead focused on the completely irrelevant fact that he needed to shave and how much she liked it.

'I can't,' she whispered, still unable to drag her eyes from his face. Then it hit her full force. He wanted her to stay, to remain in a loveless marriage, and he wanted *her* to have his child, his heir.

Disbelief robbed her of words. How could he expect her to have a child, to bring it into the world out of a sense of duty, passing on that heavy legacy to the child—her child? No, the need to be dutiful stopped here. It stopped with her.

'Can't or won't?' he demanded quickly, his voice deep and gravelly.

She took a deep breath and stood her ground, instilling as much courage into her voice as possible. This was one battle he would lose. 'I will not have your child, Kazim.'

'But that is why you are here in Barazbin.' Incredulity resonated from him and she smiled. She had dared to defy and challenge the mighty Prince Kazim Al Amed of Barazbin. Not something he was used to, she was sure, but what could he do to her now? The worst had already happened.

'That is not the only reason I'm here and you know it.' Fury pumped around her now, forcing her on because, whatever the outcome, this had to be sorted—once and for all. 'I am here because you *blackmailed* me with the health of a young child, someone I care about, Kazim. How could you be so cruel?'

His jaw clenched but he said nothing and she ploughed on.

'When we talked that night in my flat, not once did you mention your need for an heir. What were you planning? To seduce me then send me away again as soon as I'd had the child?' Hurt spiked in her heart at the very thought of such a suggestion. Would he really be that hard and unfeeling? A few days ago she would have said no, but right now, as he looked at her, she wasn't at all sure.

'That's outrageous!' he protested. But she stood firm, his reaction proof enough that that was exactly what he'd planned.

As if to test her further, the wailing of the wind increased and the tent walls seemed to flap wildly, and she wondered if it would at any minute fall down around her. Just like her marriage had. Now it seemed her life was doing the same thing. For a few short days in England she'd glimpsed what could be, sampled the delights of loving, but since arriving back in Barazbin everything had fallen apart. Her dreams and shattered hopes were crushed almost beyond recognition. He'd never wanted her, not in the way she wanted him. He needed her, not as a woman, but in the same way an actor would need a prop.

'It's the truth, Kazim, and you know it.' Oh, how she wished she could storm off somewhere and give vent to her ever increasing frustration.

'Truth seems to be something you are not familiar with.' He spoke softly, his voice lowered and his inky black eyes fixing hers with a piercing gaze. 'From the minute I saw you in that club, you have lied to me. You can't deny that, Amber. Everything you have said has been wrapped in deceit.'

'That is not true,' she gasped, remembering the way she'd allowed him to jump to conclusions about the money. She'd let him assume she'd spent it all, had frittered it away on frivolous things. 'I'm not in the wrong. You're the one who always made assumptions because His Royal Highness is always right, no matter what.'

'Now you are talking nonsense.' He shot the words out, his anger at her ridicule obvious.

'I'm speaking the truth and you know it. You deceived me about the reason I had to return here with you, not to mention the callous blackmail tactics you employed.' The tent seemed to bow inwards to them, as if the wind wanted to join in, but she didn't take her eyes from his.

'This has gone on long enough,' Kazim snapped as fury and frustration boiled over inside him. As far as he was concerned, there was nothing more to discuss. They were married and that marriage would produce the heir he needed.

He watched as Amber took in a deep breath. He'd never met such a challenging woman. Neither had he met a woman he wanted so much. Even now, with furious words flying between them and the undisguised mistrust radiating from her, he still desired her.

'Yes, it has and as soon as I can I am leaving. I want to go back to my flat in Paris, and to start my art course. I want my life back, Kazim. I will not be a part of your power games.'

'Strong words for a woman in such a weak position.'

'I'm not the one who needs the heir,' she said slowly, her delicate brows raised in mockery. 'Which I think will put you in the weak position. And yes, I intend to be strong.'

'You are back in Barazbin as my wife, truly my wife.' He watched as annoyance flashed across her face. 'That, at least, is something we can build on.'

'What is?'

'The attraction we have for one another. You can't deny that, even now. You don't want me to kiss you?' He watched her eyes turn a deeper brown and become heavy, but as her lips pressed together he saw her expression change, as if she'd just stepped behind a protective barrier. A wall meant to keep him out.

'I most certainly do not,' she retorted as she walked away.

She wasn't getting away with it that easily. If he had to face up to things then so did she. Love was what she'd called the simmering tension that stretched tautly between them every second they were together. He called it lust.

'Prove it,' he said as he followed her, grabbing hold of her arm and pulling her against

him, the silk of her *abaya* whispering softly.
Her breasts pressed against his chest and a hot
stab of lust hurtled through him. All he was
doing was proving *he* was the one attracted to
her, while she remained rigid in his arms. Unyielding and unrelenting.

'No, I will not.' Each word was razor-sharp
and she glared up at him.

The challenge was too much.

'Then I will.'

With that his lips claimed hers in a demanding kiss, one that made his pulse race. Beneath
his lips, hers remained still and pressed tightly
shut, but as his hand plunged into the softness
of her hair they parted and a sigh escaped. His
heart rate rocketed and desire thumped in his
blood.

He'd proved his point. It didn't matter how
much she protested, she wanted him. She was
his. He should stop now, should pull back and
let her know he'd won, but he couldn't. He didn't
want to. Hot need for her was rushing through
him and as she sighed against his lips once
more, pressing her body harder against him,
he knew he was lost.

'How can this be so right when everything
else is wrong?' she whispered as she pulled back
to look up at him, her breathing hard and fast,
her eyes like molten gold and heavy with desire.

He couldn't answer her, not when he didn't even know why himself. He'd never known such an overwhelming need before, such all consuming passion that had the power to render anything else inconsequential. 'All that matters at the moment is kissing you,' he said in a hoarse whisper as he ran his fingers once again through her hair before angling her head so that he could kiss her deeper and harder than ever. 'I don't care about duty, the wind or the rebels. All I care about is kissing you.'

Amber was intoxicating and Kazim was well and truly lost. Could it be that he was hers, that he would for ever be hers?

'Kazim, I...' Her voice was barely above a whisper as she looked up at him, her brown eyes full of the same desire that thudded in his veins. 'I can't...we mustn't.'

'We should,' he said in a low rumble, unable to deny his need for her any longer. 'And we will.'

With that he moved her towards the low bed, laid her down against the array of cushions and covered her body with his. She wrapped her arms around his neck, pulling him down to her, all protest and fight gone from her glorious body.

'We shouldn't,' she said in a husky whisper as she spread her palms against his back, which only increased the heated hardness of his body. The very fact that she still wanted him, that, despite her protests, she couldn't stop kissing and touching him, made him want her all the more.

Urgency filled Amber's kiss as she pulled him down closer to her. She wanted him. She knew that doing this would only make it harder to leave, but she was powerless to resist. She shouldn't, but she couldn't help herself. It was madness—total madness.

Kazim's hands deftly worked to remove the daring red *abaya* she'd dressed in until she lay on a bed of red silk, totally naked to his gaze, her whole body on fire. Eagerly he pulled his robe off, towering above her as he knelt among the cushions. He was magnificent; every honed muscle made her quiver with desire.

'Do you still think we shouldn't?' His deep voice, now a hoarse whisper, sent a shiver of anticipation racing down her spine.

She shook her head and licked her dry lips as his dark-skinned nakedness was revealed, her eyes drawn down to the evidence that, if nothing else, he desired her.

Warmth pooled between her legs and she reached out to touch him, enjoying the sudden power as he closed his eyes and groaned in pleasure. But it wasn't enough. She wanted more—much more.

As if sensing her desire, he moved and once again covered her body, this time the heat of his scorching hers. Then, with frantic need, more powerful than she'd ever experienced before, she wrapped her legs around him, encouraging him deep inside her. She lifted her hips, moving with him as a tidal wave of passion submerged them. She cried out, hearing him cry out too.

Passion slipped away and she lay naked against him, the wind blowing less wildly against the tent. Kazim had been right. The storm had blown itself out and, like the wind, her heart rate slowly became more normal.

She shouldn't have done that, shouldn't have given into the carnal lust that just one touch from him could spark. How could she leave and go back to her old life after a moment like that?

CHAPTER ELEVEN

THE JOURNEY BACK to the palace had been strained, the week in the desert abandoned. The tension had pulled them almost to breaking point. Amber still couldn't understand how they had ended up making love the previous night. Had Kazim been proving a point to her or himself? If so, what was it?

Did he want her to admit she was unable to resist him? Or was it that he could share such a moment without uttering a single word of love? He'd made it perfectly clear that love wasn't and never would be on his agenda. It was only ever going to be about duty.

As she'd argued her point last night she'd been sure she wanted to leave, but now, as the hot sun shone down on the peace of the palace gardens, she didn't know what she wanted any more. She had fallen more deeply in love with him with each passing day and, whilst she craved love, she couldn't imagine a future without him.

'I was told I'd find you here.' Kazim's deep, sexy voice broke through her tumultuous thoughts and she looked up, shielding her eyes against the sun, watching him approach.

Her heart hammered in her chest as her stomach turned over. The image he created in his white robes and headdress was overwhelming. His tanned face was so handsome her fingers itched to touch him, to caress his face and feel the slight roughness of his stubble.

But she couldn't. In that moment she realised she would be fooling herself if she stayed. She had to leave this place and this marriage, in order to keep her sanity. Her reaction to just seeing him now proved this beyond any doubt. And now was the moment to tell him. The inevitable had been delayed long enough.

She stood up, not wanting to have him tower over her, reminding her of his power. 'I must leave Barazbin. I need to go back to Paris.' She kept her voice hard and determined. The previous night in the desert had proved just how easily he could derail her.

He looked at her, his eyes searching her face, then he crossed his arms over his chest and took in a deep breath. Those seconds she waited for his response seemed like for ever.

'As you wish.' His tone was curt and his eyes sharp as he looked into hers.

Had he just agreed? Just like that, she was free? Relief washed over her and she took in a deep ragged breath, amazed how easy it had been. Then hurt rattled in. He thought so little of her he was willing to let her go, to leave for good.

'I need to be back in Paris for when Annie and Claude arrive home.' She pressed her palm hard against her collarbone, as if doing so would keep in all the hurt that threatened to escape, to make itself known to him.

She saw his jaw clench. 'Will you stay in Paris?' His voice was a guttural growl, reminding her of the first rumbles of thunder.

Was he asking if she intended ever to return to Barazbin? Was that why he'd accepted her request so calmly, because he thought it would be a visit? Whatever the reason, she had to make it clear.

'Yes, Kazim,' she said, hating the slight falter in her voice. 'I will be staying in Paris—for good.' She looked into his eyes and again the seconds ticked by, but she couldn't remain like that and she lowered her gaze, breaking the connection.

He pressed his lips together and nodded in acceptance of what she'd just said. The sun hurt her eyes and she had trouble seeing his face clearly, unable to read his expression. Why, after all that had happened in the desert, was he allowing her to walk out on him?

She hadn't expected this, but it hurt. She loved him—so much it was painful, and he was totally devoid of any emotion, any reaction to the news that she was leaving him. She swallowed down hard as tears threatened her. Quickly, she used the fierceness of the sun as an excuse. 'That sun is so bright, I can hardly see you.'

'I know,' he said calmly, his eyes never leaving her face.

What did he know? That her heart was breaking just to say those words? That she loved him so much she had to leave? Frantically, she searched for something else to say, anything that would take her mind from the pain of saying goodbye.

'What about Annie and Claude? Have you any news from them?' A little edge of desperation crept into her voice. She hadn't spoken to Annie and was nervous as to what she would say, especially about her marriage. Shamefaced, she realised that if she'd lied to Kazim by omission she'd also lied to Annie the same way.

'They are due to return from America next week, all being well.' He walked along the pathway that staked its claim boldly through the garden. He broke the eye contact that had seen every move she'd made, every emotion that had crossed her face.

After a few paces he stopped, his back to her, pausing as if he wanted to say something else. She waited. Nothing.

She looked at him, drinking him in as if it was the last time she'd see him, trying to imprint him on her memory, her heart.

'Good, that will give me time to get the flat in order before they return,' she said brightly—a little too brightly if his sudden glance at her was anything to go by. 'I'd like to leave as soon as possible.'

Kazim knew what she said made sense. Their marriage should never have been revived. It had been a mistake for him to ever think of getting her back, they were so wrong for one another. Yes, he might desire her with a raging fire more wicked than the desert heat, but that wasn't a foundation on which to build his marriage and the future of his kingdom. Still, her eagerness to leave hurt.

'I have a plane ready. You will leave at once.' He couldn't look at her and instead feigned interest in the plants that flowered in the garden, with little regard for the anguish he felt deep inside. That pain was something he couldn't yet analyse; all he could do was lock it away, pretend it didn't exist.

'You have a plane ready?' The shock was more than evident in her voice and he closed his eyes against the wave of nausea that thrashed his body. He nodded his answer, unable to trust his voice to work, and remained with his back to her. He had to appear in control and right now he wasn't.

'How? Why?' she said, stammering slightly over the words.

'Because you are right,' he said as he whirled round to face her. He could at least say these words to her face—the beautiful face he would never forget. 'We should never have got married and divorce is, as you suggested, the only option.'

He watched the soft skin of her throat, skin his lips had caressed, move as she gulped back her shock. Her eyes widened. She took a step towards him, her hand almost reaching out, then she snapped it back against her stomach, as if she too was in pain. She nodded her head slowly, the sun gleaming in her raven-black hair, and stepped back several paces. Back and away from him, he felt her retreat, felt it in the tight band that crushed his chest, threatening to suffocate him.

'Divorce,' she said firmly. 'Of course. It is

the only option and the one I wanted that very first night you found me in Paris.'

It was what he now had to do. Recent discussion with his officials, those who helped him rule his country, had made his options clear. He had to let her go. 'We have no choice in the matter now, Amber.'

'We don't?' Her delicate brows drew together in confusion.

He sighed, wishing she could at least, just once, own up to her lies and deceit.

'Not any more.' He let the words hang between them, waited as the stillness of the garden captured them. He saw her lips form the word 'why', but didn't hear it. She was speechless with shock. Just as when he'd been told what he should do, but now he had to be firm, use a hard voice, anything to keep at bay the fire of desire that raged inside him.

'Your past has caught up with you.' Every muscle in his body tightened as he said the words that would finish their marriage for ever.

'My what?' She flung the question at him full force.

'It has come to the attention of officials here at the palace exactly where you worked whilst you were in Paris.' He fought hard to keep his voice calm, still humiliated from being told just what she'd been up to. She'd made a fool of him.

'I was a waitress!' she said, interrupting his explanation—one he still found hard to believe, but the evidence had been put before him. The decision was no longer only his. He was now doing his duty. As the only heir to Barazbin, he had no option, no other choice. They couldn't remain married and that was before he took her activities with her father into consideration.

'I have told them exactly that. I defended you, Amber.' Strangely, after every lie had been exposed, he did believe she had only been waitressing.

'Why?' Her voice was hardly above a whisper as she spoke.

'That I can handle. That I can sort. But it is not just that, Amber,' he said quietly, unable to believe how events had unfolded since their return from the desert. There, as the wind had calmed its fury, he'd thought they had made a truce. But he'd been wrong. 'It is your involvement with the rebels—you knew that attack was going to happen.'

She shook her head fiercely. 'No, not that. I don't know anything about it.'

'That is not what the evidence suggests,' he said and walked towards her, unable to help himself. He balled his hands into fists at his sides, trying to keep from touching her. Her gaze darted to the movement then back to his face, questions lingering in her eyes.

'B-but...' she stammered then shook her head as if knowing that any form of defence would be useless.

'I want you to go, leave Barazbin. Divorce is the only option and, for my people to consider that, they must have more than sufficient evidence against you.' He couldn't forgive her part in the rebel attacks. She had to go. The marriage had to end.

'So, I am no longer fit to be your princess,' she said haughtily. 'No longer fit to be the mother of the heir of Barazbin and all because of lies. Lies that aren't mine, Kazim.'

'I can't forgive what you have done to my people. There is no way back from that.' He clenched his jaw against the hurt of her betrayal, wanting only to have her gone from his kingdom and his life.

She shook her head. 'It's lies—all lies.'

He couldn't say anything to that and closed his eyes briefly against the tidal wave of strange emotions that crashed against him, demanding his attention. When he did open his eyes she was watching him, her face marred by confusion. Once again he'd hurt her, but this time it really was out of a sense of duty instead of the cowardly panic that had seized him on their wedding night.

'Is this your duty too, Kazim?' she said tartly, her chin lifting in defiance, making her more elegant than ever. 'Are you following orders or do you hate me that much?'

'I don't hate you, Amber,' he said more softly and gripped his hands harder into tight fists. He mustn't weaken his resolve. He had to be firm and tell her. 'Your reputation has been brought into question and against that I stood firmly with you. As for the rest, there isn't any choice; you might as well have attacked me personally. I have to do my duty, honour my kingdom. I cannot defend what you did, not ever.'

'Cannot or will not?' She glared at him, her eyes sparking with gold, highlighting her anger.

'We both know our marriage isn't a love match and, in light of current circumstances, it can't go on.' Now he sounded just like those men who had informed him, as his father looked on, that he must get rid of his wife. Cold and unyielding.

He didn't want to send her away; he wanted her to stay. He'd glimpsed last night what they could have had, how it could have been. But that was over now. He could never forgive her involvement in the attacks, however small it might have been. All he wanted was to see her leave—right now.

Amber crumbled inside, her heart shattering into tiny shards that threatened to lacerate every part of her body. A body that craved Kazim, even now. She couldn't move, couldn't say a word. Shock had rooted her to the spot as surely as if she were one of the plants around her, and the hot sun beat down relentlessly, sapping every last bit of strength from her.

She shook her head, denying what was blatantly obvious. He didn't want her and was probably glad of that final bit of evidence that had condemned her and their marriage. He'd even organised a plane to get her away from him as fast as possible. This was worse—far worse—than what he'd done to her on their wedding night. This was more than rejection. It was total annihilation of her and the love she had for him.

She closed her eyes against the memory of the moment she'd told him she loved him. *Love is a fool's indulgence.* His words haunted her and she snapped her eyes open. She couldn't go there now. Not yet. Not while he still stood watching her. Did he have no mercy at all?

'If you'll excuse me, I need to pack.' He looked startled at her words. But what had he expected her to do? Beg and plead? Why should she when he couldn't even defend her against the decision of his officials? He hadn't even waited to hear her side of the story. He'd just decided she was guilty, believing those around him instead. 'I will be ready to leave in an hour.'

More like five minutes. The thought of staying for an hour almost knocked her breath away, but she needed time alone to compose herself, to regroup her emotions. If she was leaving she would do it with her head held high. Whatever charges had been made against her, she was innocent and she would leave this beautiful palace with as much dignity as possible.

'Very well,' he said then turned and marched away, his white robes seeming to trail after him. She watched him go, his fast pace suggesting he couldn't get away from her quickly enough. Finally he disappeared into the grand archway that led to his offices. Was he now reporting back to those who'd believed she was little better than a traitor?

True to her word, one hour later Kazim watched as Amber walked from the palace to the waiting car. Her face was a mask, hiding all her emotions. Her body, now dressed in jeans and a soft white blouse, seemed to call to his and he gritted his teeth against the stab of desire that raced through him, reminding him of the hours they'd spent making love.

Desire would not rule his country. Strong will and determination would. It was his destiny, his duty, and Amber was not and never should have been part of it.

She stopped by the car and turned to face him as he stood on the steps of the palace. He kept his eyes hard as he looked into hers, glad of the distance that now prevented him from reaching for her. That tightness clamped a little harder round his chest as her eyes met his and for a moment it was as if it was only them, nobody else existed.

This wasn't helping at all. 'Goodbye, Amber.'

She didn't say anything. She just looked at him, head held high, body full of regal composure. Then she slipped her sunglasses on and for a moment longer watched him before getting into the car.

The driver shut the door; the noise, though hardly audible, banged in Kazim's head painfully. He remained tall and strong, not wanting anyone to know the agony that stabbed at him now, as if someone was actually putting a knife into his heart.

The car moved away from the palace; the darkened windows meant it wasn't possible to see Amber, to see if she felt the knife too. But why would she, when she'd wanted to leave all along? He took a deep breath and the pain intensified. Deep down he knew why, but he couldn't admit it now. Not whilst those who'd exposed her lies stood watching nearby. He had to remain focused. He had a duty to his people, his country and, as hard as it was to admit, to his father. Anything else was unthinkable.

CHAPTER TWELVE

SUMMER IN PARIS was nowhere near as hot as Barazbin, but relief from the heat scarcely made up for the pain in her heart. For two whole days Amber had given into despair and had stayed in the flat, not wanting food, not wanting anything other than Kazim. Finally, sense had prevailed.

This morning she had thrown open the windows of the flat, sounds from the streets below filtering in. Spurred on by the fact that Annie and Claude would soon be home, she'd set about bringing life back to the tired rooms.

Next she moved onto the task she'd been putting off—unpacking. She was back from Barazbin for good and it was past time to sort through everything she'd hastily packed a few days earlier. As she reached into the bottom of the case, her fingers touched the red silk of her *abaya*— the one she'd been wearing on that last night with Kazim, the one she'd allowed herself to bring home so that she could remember him.

Each time she saw that silk it would either take her back to the moments when he'd coldly accused her of lying, or to the moment when he'd seductively removed every trace of it from her body before making her his, one last time.

As if in slow motion she stood and lifted the garment up against her. She inhaled deeply, smelling the desert—and Kazim.

Why did she have to love him so intensely and so painfully?

That night in the desert had been a mixture of anguish and ecstasy. He'd refused to acknowledge her love, but his body had welcomed it. Then it had all changed by the time they'd returned to the palace. He'd become cold and distant.

She closed her eyes against the memory of the moment she'd left the palace. He'd been like a statue, firm and resolute. He had no emotion for her, not even sympathy, and she'd been forced to retreat behind her sunglasses as tears had welled in her eyes. Tears she would never let him see.

When he'd told her why she had to go it was obvious he was saying it out of duty. He was ending their marriage because of duty to his kingdom.

Well, so be it. He'd made his choice, one that was probably for the best. After all, she'd made it clear from the start she hadn't wanted to return to Barazbin. All that existed between them was passion. Her love for him had to stay buried. She had to think of it as a love affair, a wild and passionate few days that had come to an end.

It was time to move on.

There had been no word from him since she'd left. Nothing. Over the last few days she had come to accept that what they'd shared had been driven by lust—certainly on Kazim's part. Lust that had burnt itself out, finally overridden by duty.

But hadn't he married her out of duty? She frowned. If duty had been his motivation wouldn't he have wanted the marriage to work? Her head felt heavy with confusion. Even when she wasn't with him he could still muddle everything.

'Enough!' She spoke firmly to her reflection as she brushed her hair and scraped it up into a ponytail.

She needed to focus her attention on more important matters. In a few days Annie and Claude would be back. Her life could return to normal and the last few weeks would fade into a dreamlike status.

But it isn't what I want. She pulled hard to tighten her ponytail but the sudden jolt of pain wasn't nearly as sharp as the one that ripped through her heart each time she thought of Kazim.

She closed her eyes against that pain. *This is the last time. You have to move on.* She opened her eyes and glared at her reflection. 'Stop this.'

There would be time enough to sort the unpacking tomorrow. Right now she felt enclosed; the short amount of time back in the desert had reminded her to be appreciative of space—and right now that was what she needed.

As if on a mission, she grabbed her bag and, feeling slightly liberated, opened the door of the flat, humming as she quickly went down the stairs. It was gloomy in the corridor but sunlight streamed in as soon as she opened the old door that Kazim had been so disgusted with.

'Oh!' she gasped, shock hurtling at her, and stepped back a pace. Had her imagination just done that? She blinked a few times and looked again. Kazim *was* standing on the street, a few steps below her, as large as life.

'What have you come for this time? You've already made it clear that our marriage is over,' she snapped angrily at him. How dare he come back and upset the delicate balance she'd finally managed to achieve?

He moved towards her, his casual Western clothes allowing him to blend in with everyone on the street—almost. The wild untamed power he'd always radiated was still evident and his shiny black hair and handsome features meant he would never completely blend in; even in Barazbin he'd stood out. Just as he had when he'd found her at the club. The aura of power that surrounded him was undeniable.

Neither was she immune to him. Her heart rate accelerated, racing wildly, and, although she tried to tell herself it was nothing more than the trauma of seeing him on her doorstep, she knew it was him. Her husband.

She cursed herself for not being stronger. But how could she quash her love for him? It was almost impossible, even when it was obvious that he would never love in return.

'We need to talk, Amber.' Eyes as black as midnight slipped quickly down her body and she fought hard against the sensation of tingles, as if he'd actually touched her. Did he have to do that, look at her with hot desire in his eyes whilst his voice sounded so aloof?

'I don't think so, Kazim.' A prickle of indignation ran down her spine and she stood taller, thankful for her position above him on the steps. It made her feel in charge. In control. 'You've said it all.'

'No.' He moved up a step. Closer to her, but still leaving her able to look down on him. 'No,

I said only what I should have said, what it was my duty to say.'

She fumbled absently with the strap of her handbag and scrunched her eyes in confusion. Why did he have to talk in riddles all the time? Couldn't he just say what he needed and go?

What it was my duty to say. The words sank in, seeping into her heart, and she knew she couldn't allow him to soften her mood. She shook her head in denial.

'Can we go inside, Amber?' he said as he looked at his watch, the movement snagging her attention. 'I only have a short time.'

That admission annoyed her more than she cared to admit. Once she'd left his palace she'd never thought she'd have to face him again and now here he was, demanding time with her and setting boundaries once again.

'So in that short time you thought you'd just stop by and upset my life all over again, did you?'

He looked shamefaced as she glared down at him and her fingers suddenly gripped tightly onto her handbag as if it were a lifeline. Then his eyes met hers and he moved up a step, bringing them level with one another, and she felt the balance slightly shift.

Nothing else seemed to exist; the daily sounds

of life in Paris became muted, her mind focused totally on him.

'We can't discuss this here,' he said, his voice deep and firm. 'Let's go inside.'

'Sorry, Kazim, I have nothing to say to you.' She tried hard to sound upbeat and happy, when really she was dissolving inside. 'All communication should now be through my solicitor.'

'Do you have a solicitor?' His voice rose in question, his eyes glittering like ice crystals in the winter sun.

'Not yet.' She growled the words at him, angry that he could even think he could turn up and try to undermine her.

'Then how can I communicate with your solicitor?'

'Don't be facetious.' Was he making fun of her, tormenting her on a new level? She could hardly control the buzz of attraction that raced through her, mixing with the hurt and anger at his continued rejection of her.

'Amber…' He reached out to take her arm and she jumped back, scalded by the very thought of his touch.

'Don't, Kazim, don't. In fact, just go.' She turned and opened the door of the flat, all thought of her earlier decision to go out and shop gone. She needed to escape him and the way his gaze, so dark and lingering, still affected her. All she wanted was to lock the door against him and her marriage.

'Not until you've heard what I have to say and if it means saying it here on the street, I will.' His words were low but steely, firm with determination, and she knew she had little choice left.

She shook her head in a small movement of denial. If he was going to press home his point about duty and hurl accusations of deceit at her she couldn't take it any more. She'd heard enough.

She looked into his eyes and her heart almost stopped beating. In their depths she saw something she'd never seen before—uncertainty. It unnerved her and she wasn't even sure if she really wanted to hear what he had to say. She didn't want his decision to end the marriage re-affirmed yet again. What good would that do either of them?

'Five minutes.' She relented and opened the door. Without a backward glance to see if he was following, she marched back up to her flat.

'It may take a little longer than that.' His deep voice drifted up to her and her body reacted to the sensuous undercurrent of sexiness that seemed to be weaved into every word.

She stopped by her front door. Did he really think he could charm her so easily? 'Say what you have to, Kazim, then leave. For good.'

She walked into the small flat and dropped her handbag down onto the kitchen worktop. The stillness of the flat careered into her turmoil. She couldn't get over how quiet the place was without Annie and Claude, and Kazim's brooding presence only intensified it.

She heard him shut the door and her mind raced back to the moment in the dressing room of the club. Was it really only a few weeks ago? He'd stood resolutely against the door, barring her exit and forcing her to listen. She turned to face him and a little smile tugged at her lips despite the wild array of emotions rushing through her. With his arms folded across his chest, he stood with his back to the door, his body completely overwhelming the small corridor.

'Come through,' she said and led the way into the small living room, which was considerably lighter than the hallway. She hoped he would appear less intimidating there, but as he entered the room she knew it was useless. The power of his presence would never be overruled. He was a born leader, a man who exuded command and, to her shame, she could hardly drag her gaze from him.

He looked at his watch again and irritation crept over her. 'Okay, what is so important, Kazim?'

'I want you to come back to Barazbin.' His

firm words were loaded with intent and for a moment left her speechless. This couldn't be happening, not again.

'Why? Is the great Kazim Al Amed not able to get the divorce he wants?' She tried really hard to keep the spike of hurt from sounding in her voice, but it was as if he was twisting a knife in her heart. Why did he have to be so cruel and why did she have to allow it to hurt so much?

What was worse was that she knew if he just said the right words that she'd go. But he would never do that. Kazim didn't do love. For some reason unknown to her, he didn't want to allow her love into his heart, his life. He hadn't when they'd married and he certainly hadn't when she'd told him she loved him. He'd thrown it back at her.

She whirled round and marched back to the door of the flat and opened it, glad now she'd made him move away from it. At least this way he didn't have control of the situation.

'No,' she said as an ice-cold sensation slid over her. 'You've said what you needed to, now go.'

He stood in the doorway of the living room, sunlight flooding in behind him, and she glared at him, her breathing deep and hard, determined not to be distracted by him. For a moment he looked at her, his black eyes almost piercing into her soul, and she wondered if he could read the confusion within her.

'You are wrong about the divorce,' he said slowly and took a step towards her, but she held her ground and stood holding onto the door of the flat. 'After what was revealed about you, divorce was the only option to be considered.'

'Ah, yes, back to duty again. Correct me if I'm wrong, Kazim, but haven't we already had this conversation?'

'Yes, Amber, we have.' He took another step closer and she swallowed hard. She had to remain calm. 'And it is duty that has brought me back to you.'

Why couldn't it have been love?

Kazim took another step towards her and reached for her hand, firmly but slowly peeling her fingers away from the door. He wasn't going anywhere yet.

Her eyes widened in surprise and for a moment he thought he saw the same spark of desire he felt just from touching her mirrored in her eyes. She'd had that effect on him since the very first time they'd met but he'd been too proud to acknowledge it. Too determined to deny it.

'What duty?' Her voice was barely above a whisper as he shut the door quietly, his every move full of purpose. He looked down at her and the rush of desire he'd known the first night of their marriage resurfaced, but this time he didn't want to push it harshly to one side. He wanted to face it, to explore it.

'My duty as your husband.' He took one more step towards her, bringing her so close he could have wrapped his arms around her at any moment. She smelt good and he breathed her scent in. 'A duty I failed in.'

'Did you?' She looked up as she asked the question in a tremulous whisper.

He couldn't help himself as he reached out and smoothed her hair back from her face. The sigh that escaped her lips spurred him on. She was not immune to him, despite the hard bravado she hid behind.

The attraction that had simmered between them from the very first moment their eyes had met was still there and much more intense. He could feel the tension emanating from her—she still desired him and it gave him the courage he needed to face the most difficult thing he'd ever done.

'Yes.' His voice sounded gravelly to his ears as he looked down at her. 'I allowed the judgement of others to colour my views, allowed them to taint your name. I failed you.'

The grief he'd experienced after she'd left Barazbin rushed back at him. He hadn't expected to feel such pain or to know that raw and mysterious emotion of abandonment and rejection, but he had. With her head held high she'd walked out of his palace and his life without a second glance. She'd turned the tables so completely that as soon as she'd gone he'd ridden out into the desert like a man possessed to shout his anger and his pain into the wind.

'And now you believe me?' Her eyes searched his face, hope shining from them, and that all too familiar band of tightness gripped his chest.

'I do,' he said as his fingers slid through her hair, the softness almost like silk. 'Very quickly your father's web of deceit unravelled, exposing your innocence. In fact he has confessed all. His misguided loyalty to you led him along the wrong path.'

'And that's it?' She tried to step away from him but the wall was at her back. The gesture of moving away from him rang alarm bells in his head. This was not going according to plan. He believed her, he'd come to apologise. What more did she want from him?

'What else do you want?' Frustration made his question harsher than he'd intended.

'It's not enough, Kazim, not now, not ever.' She caught hold of his hand, stilled the subconscious movement of his fingers through her hair. 'I can never be what you want me to be.'

He dropped his hand to his side, another stab of rejection hurtling at him. She didn't want him to touch her. The angry glare in her eyes, which had replaced that brief glimpse of hope, told him that. 'So, tell me, what is it I want?'

'A woman who will be at your side as you rule Barazbin, a woman who will produce the heir required, but, above all, one who is dutiful and has a completely untarnished reputation.' She paused, as if waiting for him to deny those words. 'I am not that woman, Kazim.'

He turned and walked back into the living room, needing the space, needing to distance himself momentarily from her. He pressed his hand over his eyes, his thumb and finger pressing at his temples, trying to ease the pain in his head.

Behind him, she remained silent and he knew he had to open up completely. If he wanted her, he had to do this; if not he was failing himself as well as her. His heart thumped hard against his ribcage. What if she threw it back at him? Now he knew how she had felt on their wedding night and again in the desert. She'd braved his rejection not once, but twice, and he couldn't face hers once. What sort of coward did that make him?

Slowly he turned and that tightness crushed his chest harder. It was as if his love for her was squeezing the life out of him. *Love.* He'd finally used the word, in thought at least. But what would she do if he said it out loud? Coldly reject him, as he had rejected her? It would be all he deserved.

He turned and stalked across the room, overwhelmed by the smallness of it and the magnitude of what he'd just realised. He had to say it aloud, had to face the consequences of what he'd done. He crossed the small room again, wishing he could be still and tell her. Was this why his father had been a bully—to hide from himself?

Amber watched Kazim pace back and forth across the living room. Just for a moment she allowed hope to soar inside her as he looked down at her, the ebony depths of his eyes full of more than just passion and desire. She dared to hope, dared to believe he loved her. But then he marched away and her heart sank lower than it had ever gone.

'I can't ever go back, Kazim,' she said, forcing her voice to be calm and neutral. 'I am not the woman you need.'

'No.' He turned and focused his gaze on her. 'You are more—much more.'

She drew in a breath that seemed to cut her throat and looked at him. The wild and untameable man she'd said her vows to was clearly on show, standing before her. The hungry look in his eyes made her stomach flip and her knees go weak.

She didn't dare speak, but inside she was urging him on, desperate to know and yet certain she couldn't ever know what he meant.

'You are my wife, Amber.' He didn't move, as if doing so would stop the words. 'And I love you.'

Inside her head she could hear her heart thumping more slowly and in her chest her breathing turned shallow—too shallow. She couldn't move, couldn't say a word, scarcely able to believe what she'd just heard.

He doesn't mean it. How could he mean it after what he'd told her in the desert? It was just another way to charm her into doing what he wanted.

He strode towards her and all she could do was watch. He caught hold of her face in his large warm hands but still it all had a dream-like feeling.

'It's too late,' she whispered, almost trance-like.

'Too late?' He drew in a sharp breath as she spoke and looked at her, his eyes full of love and passion.

'I can never be what you need.'

'You are everything I need—and more.' He

dropped his hands to take hold of her arms, keeping her before him, preventing any escape.

Still as if in a dream, she watched as he lowered his head. Lightly his lips brushed over hers and she closed her eyes, surrendering to the moment. But it didn't come; he pulled back. Her eyes opened to look into his.

'I've been a fool—a blind fool,' he said so gently she wanted to cry. 'I have been running from you and your love for too long. I don't want to run any more.'

She shook her head in disbelief, words failing her.

'I was afraid to love, afraid that if I did I would hurt you, just as my father hurt my mother.'

'You think you'll be the same?' How could he ever have thought such a thing? 'That would never happen.'

He pulled her to him and she held her breath, waiting, wanting to hear him say what she saw in his eyes.

'I love you, Amber. You are my princess and wherever you are, whatever you are doing, I want to be there.'

'Wherever?' She whispered the word so quietly she hardly heard it herself.

'Yes, Amber, I will give up everything for you.' He kissed her then, so deeply she wondered if she'd ever breathe again, but as Kazim's arms wrapped around her she knew she'd found what she wanted and it didn't matter where they were, they would always have that. They would always love one another.

'I've lived all my life in fear of being like my father. I didn't want to break your spirit the way he broke my mother's. I just couldn't take that risk.'

'All along you've thought that?' She looked up at him, wanting to kiss his pain away.

'Yes. Can you forgive me?'

Her body melted at the love and desire that was openly shining in his eyes. 'Your love is all I have ever wanted, Kazim, but I would never make you give up what you were born to do.'

'I was born to love you.' He pressed his lips against her forehead and pulled her close. She heard his heart beating as hard and loud as hers, beating in unison with their love.

'I love you, Kazim, with all my heart. I was born to be your princess, so take me home.' He put her at arm's length and looked into her eyes.

'I can't do that,' he said with a new gentleness in his voice and she smiled coyly at him.

'Sorry, I forgot you only had a short time; you have to be somewhere else.'

'No,' he said, brushing his lips over hers, setting fire to her body as the embers of passion rose to life once more. 'The only place I have to be is with the woman I love, but you have a friend returning from America, so we'll stay here until they are settled.'

'Here?' Incredulity filled her voice. 'You'll stay here?'

'Wherever you are, Amber, is where I want to be.'

He pulled her into his arms and, as she looked up at him, kissed her lips with so much passion and love. 'I love you, Kazim, and always have.'

He smiled at her. 'I have loved you since we first met, but I was just too proud and stubborn to realise it. I should never have listened to those who were against you. I should have listened to my heart. Can you ever forgive me?'

'It might take some time,' she teased. 'But yes, I think I can.'

EPILOGUE

Eighteen months later

AMBER HAD BEEN so happy she thought that nothing could top it. Returning to Barazbin with Kazim had been like a dream come true. Not once since he'd told her he loved her had a day gone by when he hadn't said it again.

She walked out onto the balcony to join Kazim, who was enjoying a rare moment of peace. He smiled and pulled her close against him. 'You look amazing,' he said as he brushed his lips lightly over hers. 'Motherhood suits you.'

'Our son has made a difference to so many,' she teased lightly. 'Your father is a different man.'

'My father and I have both dealt with demons in our past and are stronger for it, but I never want my son to go through what I did.' He looked at her intently.

'That will never happen, Kazim.' She smiled up at him. 'But we will be in trouble with your father if we don't attend this evening's festivities.'

'Peace in our land is a cause for celebration and it is thanks to your father. He may have acted wrongly, but it was your honour he sought to defend. Since then he has worked tirelessly to expose the rebel leaders. I owe him much.'

'It means so much to me that you forgave him.' Amber had been stunned to discover her father's involvement with the rebels but, even more so, that he was doing it in a bid to punish Kazim for rejecting her. He'd been avenging her honour.

'I have a surprise for you this evening,' he said as he walked back into the luxury of their suite. 'But first we need to celebrate with everyone.'

As they entered the opulence of the hall the celebrations began. She loved the dancing and laughter, and very soon she was caught up in the atmosphere of the evening. Kazim, who had been talking to others, moved back to her side.

'Hasim is here.' Kazim's words had her scanning the room. If Hasim was here, would Annie be too? She'd missed her friend so much.

She looked up at Kazim. 'And Annie? Is she here too?'

'She's here.' He smiled at her, his dark eyes

full of happiness. 'Now go, catch up with her, or whatever it is you ladies do.'

'I love you, Kazim.' She pressed her palm against his cheek, wishing they were alone and that she could show him just how much.

* * * * *

LARGER-PRINT BOOKS!

GET 2 FREE LARGER-PRINT NOVELS PLUS

2 FREE GIFTS!

⊕HARLEQUIN®

Romance

From the Heart, For the Heart

YES! Please send me 2 FREE LARGER-PRINT Harlequin® Romance novels and my 2 FREE gifts (gifts are worth about $10). After receiving them, if I don't wish to receive any more books, I can return the shipping statement marked "cancel." If I don't cancel, I will receive 4 brand-new novels every month and be billed just $4.84 per book in the U.S. or $5.24 per book in Canada. That's a savings of at least 19% off the cover price! It's quite a bargain! Shipping and handling is just 50¢ per book in the U.S. and 75¢ per book in Canada.* I understand that accepting the 2 free books and gifts places me under no obligation to buy anything. I can always return a shipment and cancel at any time. Even if I never buy another book, the two free books and gifts are mine to keep forever.

119/319 HDN F43Y

Name	(PLEASE PRINT)

Address	Apt. #

City	State/Prov.	Zip/Postal Code

Signature (if under 18, a parent or guardian must sign)

Mail to the **Harlequin® Reader Service:**
IN U.S.A.: P.O. Box 1867, Buffalo, NY 14240-1867
IN CANADA: P.O. Box 609, Fort Erie, Ontario L2A 5X3
Want to try two free books from another line?
Call 1-800-873-8635 or visit www.ReaderService.com.

* Terms and prices subject to change without notice. Prices do not include applicable taxes. Sales tax applicable in N.Y. Canadian residents will be charged applicable taxes. Offer not valid in Quebec. This offer is limited to one order per household. Not valid for current subscribers to Harlequin Romance Larger-Print books. All orders subject to credit approval. Credit or debit balances in a customer's account(s) may be offset by any other outstanding balance owed by or to the customer. Please allow 4 to 6 weeks for delivery. Offer available while quantities last.

Your Privacy—The Harlequin® Reader Service is committed to protecting your privacy. Our Privacy Policy is available online at www.ReaderService.com or upon request from the Harlequin Reader Service.

We make a portion of our mailing list available to reputable third parties that offer products we believe may interest you. If you prefer that we not exchange your name with third parties, or if you wish to clarify or modify your communication preferences, please visit us at www.ReaderService.com/consumerschoice or write to us at Harlequin Reader Service Preference Service, P.O. Box 9062, Buffalo, NY 14269. Include your complete name and address.

HRLP13R